Bear Holler Mountain, Copyright 2006 by Victor Vining.

ISBN: 978-0-615-25035-9

I0461655

CONTENTS

CHAPTER ONE

The Paradise Orphanage sat on sixteen acres of land in Hazeltown, just south of Belmont, a small town in northwest Georgia. It is twenty miles east of Hart.

The orphanage has six brick buildings situated on the land. There are two male dormitories, a female dormitory, a lunchroom, and administrative office.

Today is March 21, 1934 a date that would live in infamy. For today there is a jailbreak planned. It has been planned for many months, started during Christmas. These are the culprits:

Thomas (Boob) Jackson, age 13, five feet six inches tall, 140 pounds, with brown hair, brown eyes, both in front. He is always getting into trouble, placed on the orphanages top ten list.

Aubrey Jackson, age 12, brother to Boob, five feet five inches tall, 130 lbs with brown hair and brown eyes. He is believed to be the ringleader of the Grey Ghosts, a group responsible for many atrocities, such as putting frogs in the girls' restrooms. Not on the top ten most wanted list, but being watched very carefully.

Elijah Trehune, age 13, five feet seven inches tall, ears stick out, both sides. He is about 150 pounds, very quiet, too quiet, believed to be a member of the Grey Ghosts.

Sidney Trehune, age 12, sister of Elijah, five feet four inches tall, 110 pounds with blond hair, green eyes. Every-body watches her. Not thought to be a member of the Grey Ghosts. Remember their descriptions; posters will be put out upon their escape. Not that the orphanage wanted them back, but they did get money from the state for them.

It all started with the treasure map. Boob, for some reason was in the library. He was looking through the book, Treasure Island. Not being that familiar with books, he dropped it to the floor. When he picked it up he noticed a corner of the cover page was loose. Picking at it he saw that something was hidden behind the cover. He pealed it back and found a map hidden inside. He looked around to see if anyone was watching him. They were always watching him.

The librarian, Miss Juniper, was busy with another student. Boob went between two bookshelves and looked at the map. Sure enough it was a treasure map. He put it in his pocket to look at it later.

But first he had to fix the book to look like it was the same before he pealed off the top of the page. He was chewing some gum, breaking the law of course; he took it and put it between the book and the cover.

Yep, just like new, he thought. He put the book back on the shelf.

That night in the dormitory, he and

Aubrey were on Boob's bed looking at the map. It looked old and was worn in several places. It had the State of Georgia and the State of North Carolina on it. An X marked a spot on the North Carolina Mountains, a place called Bear Holler Mountain. On the bottom was signed Captain Alonzo Gonzales. He was one of the first explorers of Georgia and North Carolina. They said he had stolen gold from natives in the north Georgia Mountains and left with two of his men to North Carolina. No one knew what had happened to them after that. Now the map was here in Boobs hand and he knew what he had to do.

"We have to go find that gold." said Boob.

"How are we going to do that?" asked Aubrey

"We are going to leave this place, find that gold and live in high cotton."

"I don't want to live in high cotton, it itches." said Aubrey.

"No, we are going to be rich and no one will tell us what to do again." said Boob.

"How are we going to get away?" asked Aubrey.

"Let me think on It." said Boob.

Boob put the map under a loose board that was at the head of his bed.

"Aubrey, you have to keep this quiet, you hear, don't tell anyone." said Boob.

"I swear, I won't." he answered

Aubrey.

"Don't even tell Sidney."

"Why would I tell her?" asked Aubrey.

"Come on, you tell her everything."

"I do not!" shouted Aubrey.

"You promise?"

"I promise" said Aubrey.

Aubrey could keep a secret, but not for long.

The next day at the first recess, Aubrey was talking to Sidney by the slide.

"Sidney, guess what?" asked Aubrey.

"What"

"Boob found a treasure map and we are going to run away and be rich."

"Are you feeling hot, the sun getting to you?" asked Sidney.

"No, the sun isn't getting to me, you'll see."

"Go get some water and sit down." said Sidney.

Aubrey puffed up and left.

Sidney felt sorry for Aubrey; he believed anything Boob told him.

To get to the bottom of it she walked over to Boob, who was sitting on the bench by the schoolhouse.

"You've gone and done it again." said Sidney.

Boob looked up.

"Gone and done what?"

"You got Aubrey believing you are

leaving and going to be rich."

"Dad Burn that boy, he just can't keep his mouth shut."

"Boob, what are you talking about?

"I found this map, and we are going to leave and be rich."

"Are you crazy, everyone who has escaped has been brought back and put in the special attention room?"

"Yea, that's why this time I have to have full proof plan."

"You really are serious."

"Yes I am" answered Boob

"If you and Aubrey go so are Elijah and me."

"What, you can't"

"We go or I squeal"

"You would too"

Sidney just smiled.

Boob knew he was had, when a woman makes up her mind to do something it was like pulling a can away from a goat.

"OK, but you have to keep this secret, and for Gods sake, keep Aubrey quiet." said Boob.

Later that night, Boob and Aubrey showed Elijah the map. He was all for it.

"Let's go tonight" said Elijah.

"We have to plan first, we don't want to get caught and brought back here." said Boob

"Just be patient, I'll let you know when"

Now the gang of four was set, no turning

around. They were waiting for the right time.

It was close to Christmas, that's when the breakouts usually occurred. All were caught and brought back.

But Boob knew that security was tight around this time of year. The trick was to break out when no one was expecting it, maybe in the spring.

CHAPTER TWO

Boob was sitting in the classroom trying to pay attention, when he looked out the window and saw a traveler. A traveler was a person who had no job and went from one town to another to find work. Work was hard to find these days, with the depression and all.

The traveler was big, about the biggest man he had ever seen. He was big, not because he was eating regularly, but he was big boned. He wore faded overalls and had a railroad hat on. The kind that was round with a small lip in front. It was soft, so it fitted his head.

He was talking to the head cook by the cafeteria door.

, Miss Lynch was her name.

"Well, what do you want?" she asked.

"I was wondering if you needed any work to be done in exchange for a meal."

Miss Lynch usually told these men to go away, but he was big and looked strong, and some wood needed cutting.

"Can you chop wood?" she asked.

"Yess'um" he replied.

"See that pile over there, chop it up and I'll find something for you"

"The axe is over there by the woodpile.

"Yes'um" he said.

Just then a book was flying and hit Boob square on his head. Nearly knocked Book out of his seat. He knew where that book had come from; Miss Woodward, an expert at throwing books. He was not paying attention. He heard the other students laughing.

"Children" said Miss Woodward.

"That's not funny; Mr. Jackson was not paying attention to class."

Boob knew what was going to happen next. Miss Woodward pointed her finger at him and curled the index finger and pointed for him to come up to the front of the classroom.

Boob knew the routine by now, this wasn't his first time. He walked up to the front and Miss Woodward got out the hat. The dunce hat, it was tall and pointed, he thought it looked like a wizard's hat, but here it was called the dunce hat. For young'uns who did not pay attention in her class or was just plain stupid. He wasn't stupid so it was the latter. Miss Woodward put the hat on Boob's head. He then walked back to his seat, thinking he ought to put his name on it, after all he wore it the most.

Finally it was time for lunch. As he was walking to the front door of the classroom Miss Woodward had one final thing to say.

"Remember, Mr. Jackson, you keep that hat on all day and if you can pay attention tomorrow give it back to me."

I swear that women enjoyed Boob wearing that hat. It was like a contest between them. Miss Woodward wanted to save Boob from himself, and Boob who really didn't care about the whole thing. Miss Woodward had yet to figure this out.

He was going through the lunch line and the women behind the counter just smiled. They were used to seeing Boob with his hat.

Mrs. Opal, who was spooning out beans today said,

"Well Boob, I see you got that hat today, not paying attention again?

"Yes ma'mam, I swear that woman has eagle eyes" Miss Opal laughed.

Further down the counter he came to Mrs. Purely who smiled at him also.

"Boob, when are you going to retire that hat?"

"As soon as I get out of here." replied Boob.

"Lord that hat will be worn out by then" she laughed as she gave him some rice.

He was sitting at the lunch table with Aubrey and Elijah. Sidney had to sit at the girls table on the other side of the room. He looked across to her and saw her smiling too. It was nice to know he made so many People happy.

"Boob, when are you going to learn, pay attention." said Aubrey. Aubrey was the smart one in the family. He might grow up to be a salesman.

"If you paid attention you wouldn't have to wear that hat." he said.

"I like this hat, it makes me feel like a

king" said Boob.

Aubrey just shook his head. What was he going to do with him, but he was his brother so he had no choice but to keep him.

"Who's that?" asked Elijah.

Boob looked up from his plate and looked in the direction of where Elijah was pointing. Though the door to the kitchen you could see Miss Lynch giving a stranger some food.

"That's who I was looking at when I got caught." said Boob.

"Man he's big" said Aubrey.

"One day I will have me a hat like that." said Boob.

"You and your hats" replied Aubrey.

The man looked over to them and saw Boob with his hat on and smiled. Like he was remembering the time he had to wear one of those. He raised his right hand a little bit off the table and waved at them. Boob raised his hand in the air and waved.

"What are you doing?" asked Aubrey

"I was waving at the man."

"Never mind" replied Aubrey.

Later that night the boys were sitting around Boobs bed talking. Boob's hat was sitting proudly on his dresser drawers. That's what they are called in the south. Don't know why, guess undressed drawers wouldn't do.

"I figured out how we can get out of here and to the mountains." said Boob

"How?" asked the boys at once.

"You remember that man at the kitchen table?" asked Boob.

"Yea" they said.

"That's how we are going to do it" said Boob.

"He's going to take us with him?" asked Elijah.

"No, but he's a traveler, he rides the rails, that's how we leave, we jump on the train going to the mountains to North Carolina." smiled Boob.

"You are kidding" said Aubrey.

"No, it will work, we just have to how to get from the school to the train yards." said Boob

"Yea, we have to figure that out first" said Aubrey.

"Let me work on that" answered Boob.

But it wasn't that hard at all. It had to be done in the middle of the night. That way they had more time to get away and with less chance of someone seeing them. Simple, Boob thought. That's why he wore the hat, simple.

At breakfast the next morning he told the rest of the group about it, he knew Elijah would tell Sidney later.

"OK, let's set the day for March 21st." said Boob.

"Why the 21st." asked the rest.

"Because that's the first day of spring, and we are springing out" said Boob smiling.

13

"That's only a week" said Aubrey.

"We have to start getting some food."

"I got it" said Aubrey as he whispered to them at the table.

They all looked up when he was through and nodded their heads in agreement.

At lunch the plan began. Boob was in the lunch line in front of Mrs. Opal, when he asked her,

"Can I have some extra bread; I sure like your bread." Boob asked.

Mrs. Opal said yes and put some extra slices on his plate. Next came, Aubrey and then Elijah and Sidney. They all asked for extra bread.

"Well" said Mrs. Opal. She didn't know that the kids liked bread so much.

At the table the kids put the extra bread into a sack that Aubrey had brought. He kept it; if Boob had kept it someone would stop him and ask him what he was up to. With Aubrey, the smart one, he got away with everything.

They had decided that bread would be the best thing to take. It was hard to put rice and corn in a bag without it coming through. They did this for a week until the night had come for the escape.

CHAPTER THREE

Since the dorms didn't have any guards it wouldn't be hard to sneak out. The plan was to meet by the woods next to Dorm Two. From there they would go to the rail yard and hop a freight car.

Boob was getting dressed as Aubrey came to his bed ready to go. They went to the door, looked out, and ran to the woods. No one had seen them. It was a cool night, so the coats they had helped. After what seemed like hours, they could see Elijah and Sidney coming their way.

"This is it, you sure you want to do this?" asked Boob to them.

"Yep" said both of them.

"OK, let's go"

With that they left the Paradise Orphanage behind them, hoping they would not see it again.

"Do you know where you are going?" asked Sidney.

"Yep, the trains are that way" said Boob pointing in one direction.

"How do you know?" asked Sidney.

"Because that's where you hear the sound of the trains coming from." said Boob confidently.

"Great," answered Sidney.

They came out of the woods and sure enough there were the freight cars. Sidney just looked at Boob and shook her head.

"Which one?" asked Elijah?

"The ones headed toward the mountains" replied Boob.

"Hey, it worked the first time" said Sidney

They found an open door on a freight car they hoped was headed toward the mountains.

"How are we going to get in" asked Sidney

"We help Boob up first, and then he can grab our arms and lift us up" replied Aubrey.

With that plan they managed to get aboard.

The only light that was coming in was from the open door, the rest was in darkness.

Without warning someone jumped on and landed next to them.

"What the Hey!" the man shouted.

"What in the devil are you children doing here?"

"We are running away from the orphanage" said Elijah.

The train bumped and started to move.

"I can make a lot of money turning you kids in" said the stranger.

"Just so you don't get away."

"Turn around I'm going to tie you up.

He ordered them to stand in a circle next to each other.

He grabbed Sidney first, she started to

16

kick and bite. The stranger raised his arm to hit her when out of the dark came a shadow. It grabbed his arm, turned him around and slugged him. He was picked up and thrown out the door. He bounced for a far piece. The place he landed was not smooth; in fact there were briar bushes all around. We heard him screaming for a while.

The stranger turned around and looked at them. They were frozen. Did he want the money too? He stepped into the light coming through the door.

"That's the man who was at the orphanage." said Boob.

"It's alright kids, what are you doing here?" he asked.

"You don't want to know." said Sidney

He smiled and said,

"Tell me anyway"

"We are going to find buried treasure" said Boob

"You what?"

"We are going to find buried treasure and get rich"

He looked over at Sidney

"It's his idea, we were fools enough to come along." she said.

He sat down on the floor, crossed his legs and said,

"Let me hear the whole story."

It took a few minutes for Boob to tell it and when he was through the man didn't say anything. The first words he did say was,

"I be danged"

"I can't talk you out of this, can I?"

"No" said Boob.

"I was raised in an orphanage too. I don't blame you for not wanting to go back. But you are too young to be doing this alone. There are many more men like the one who just got off. There are good men too, just out of work; at home they have children too. I'll go with you as far as Table Rock, North Carolina. That is where you need to get off, until then do everything I tell you to do, you understand?"

"Yep" they all answered.

"Can I ask you a question?" said Sidney

"Sure"

"What's your name?"

"My legal name is James Dublin"

"But my rail name is Big Cat" he answered. They could see why, he was about six foot six and three hundred pounds. They knew if Big Cat was on their side, they would be alright.

The children stayed in a group at their end of the boxcar. They huddled together for warmth. They fell asleep to the sound of the thump, thump, and thump of the box car wheels running on the tracks

It seemed that they had hardly laid down when someone was shaking them awake.

"Come on, got to get up, we have got to go" said Big Cat.

"Huh, what?" asked Boob.

"We have to get off before Hazeltown, the railroad thumpers are there" said Big Cat.

"Railroad Thumpers?" asked Sidney.

"Railroad Men who carry bats and thump you on the head if they find you." replied Big Cat

"Where are we going?" asked Aubrey.

"We're going to jump, and hurry the place is coming up fast"

"Jump!" all of the children shouted at once

"Over here, line up"

They lined up in front of the door, watching the trees and bushes fly by. They weren't too sure about this. Elijah was in the front, not that he volunteered, it just came out that way.

"We have to do this fast, there's only a grassy area so big." said Big Cat.

"I don't know about this" said Elijah.

Big Cat was sticking his head out the door when he said,

"Alright, Now!" he shouted.

He grabbed each one by the waist and threw them out the door. He followed behind. They all bounced a couple of times, but the landing area was soft. The train went on down the tracks without them. All were alright, except Elijah who was so dizzy he was walking around in circles.

"Let's go" said Big Cat.

19

Boob, Sidney, and Aubrey began following Big Cat into a patch of woods along the tracks. Sidney looked back and saw Elijah starting to walk back across the tracks. She went back to get him and lead him into the woods. They walked about 300 yards, back into the trees. They came upon a site that amazed them. It seemed that a small village was hidden there. Not of houses, but of tents, tree limbs and of lumber.

Big Cat was walking to an area on the right side of the camp where three men were seated around a fire.

"Howdy Tin Cup" said Big Cat to man sitting at the fire.

"Well Big Cat, haven't seen you in a while" he answered.

The children were hiding behind Big Cat while peeping out to see the men.

"What have you got there?" asked Tin Cup.

"I picked these young'uns up inside a car"

"What in the world were they doing there?"

"It's a long story, I'll tell you later."

"Don't be afraid, come up to the fire and get warm" said Tin Cup to the children.

They all eagerly came forward to the warmth of the fire. They sat down on the ground in front. They looked at the three men from across the fire. Tin Cup was thin, clean shaven, except for some stubble. He wore a big floppy hat. He had small silver glasses that hung on his nose. On his right was a man who had bumps on his head, they could tell because he was bald. He had a little hair along the sides. He was thin too. On Tin Cups left was a man who had most of the hair, it needed cutting. He was a little heavier and had a mustache. Also they saw that he was wearing shoes that were too big for him. On top of that he had no socks on. He also had a pipe which he was smoking. This was the group that they had fallen in with.

"Welcome to Hobo town" said Tin Cup.

"This is Boob, and Elijah, Aubrey and "Sidney" said Sidney.

"And Sidney" finished Big Cat.

"Children you know Tin Cup, called so because he always has a tin cup on him, on his right is Knot Head, because he is always getting caught by the railroad gang and he gets thumped.

"Don't hurt none, I got a hard head" said Knot Head.

"And on his left is Shoeless because when he runs from the thumpers he runs clean out of his shoes."

"Nice to meet you" the children said.

"At least they're polite" said Tin Cup.

"And hungry?" asked Tin Cup.

"We got some food" said Aubrey taking the bag he had and opened it to take out the

21

bread.

"That looks good but maybe you would like some beans with that?" said Tin Cup.

They shook there heads yes.

"We have already ate, Shoeless get some plates and help the children" said Tin Cup.

Shoeless went into the tent and brought out four tin plates and put some beans on the plates from the kettle over the fire.

He then passed them around. They sat there and watched four kids gobble down the food.

The men looked at each other and smiled. When they were through, Shoeless said,

"Come with me to the creek, I'll show you how to wash them."

The children followed him down through the woods to the creek.

"OK, Big Cat, what's the story?"

"They ran away from an orphanage, I don't blame them there, but the reason is odd. It seems that Boob found a treasure map in a book and they got it in there heads to go and find it and be rich."

"I was on the boxcar in the rail yard at Belmont. The next thing I know they jump on board. I didn't want to scare them so I stayed in the Shadows. When we started to move, Bounty Man jumped on board, you remember him, he's the one who turned you over to the

Thumpers for cash."

"Yea, I won't forget him, so what happened next?"

"It seemed that he saw dollar signs with the young'uns and he was going to tie them up, he grabbed Sidney, bless that girl she fought for her life, be she didn't have a chance with Bounty Man. He started to hit her and you know me, Tin, I'm not one for that. So I thumped him and threw him out the door."

"Ha, Ha, Ha, I'll like to have seen that, no one deserved it more" said Tin Cup.

"What are you going to do with them?" asked Tin Cup.

"I can't turn them in Tin, and you know they don't have a chance by their selves, so I'll take them as far a Table Rock."

"Big Cat, you got too big a heart"

"They have nothing, all they have is a bag of bread." said Knot Head.

"When they get back, I'll take them down to the pile" said Big Cat.

When the children came back from the creek, Big Cat said to them,

"Follow me"

They followed him over to a pile of what appeared to be clothes, shoes and more.

"This is where we put extras or things men don't need anymore" said Big Cat.

"Look in there, find some sleeping bags, cups, plates, forks." said Big Cat.

They all dug through the pile, each one

finding what they needed.

"Come on down to the tent, later Shoeless will show you how to shake the sleeping bags at the creek; need to get the bugs out of them."

You couldn't see them for the stuff they carried. Big Cat laughed, all you could see were legs walking beneath. He would show them later how to put the stuff in the sleeping bags and tie the bag so they could carry all of it on their backs.

They spent that night in the men's tent. The men sleep outside by the fire. They were lying in the sleeping bags watching the Shadows cast by the fire dance on the tent sides.

"Boob, you awake?" asked Aubrey. "Can't sleep, I got things crawling all over me?" said Boob.

"What do you think they will do when they find us gone?"

"Celebrate mostly" answered Boob.

"No, really"

"I don't know, but I do know I don't want to go back"

"Me neither"

"Big Cat saved our lives back there" said Elijah.

"I just about had that man when he stopped him" said Sidney

The boys looked at her and smiled. Sidney didn't like that,

24

"Well, I almost had him" she replied.

They talked for a little while and one by one each feel asleep, asleep in their new surroundings and their sleeping bags.

The next morning Big Cat awoke them and told them to get ready for breakfast.

"OK, let's rise and shine" he yelled through the tent flaps.

They awoke with sleep still in their eyes and hungry enough to eat a bear. One by one each came out of the tent. When they looked down at the camp fire, hope faded. More beans. To Boob that bear was looking pretty good.

"Don't be so sad looking" said Shoeless.

"For lunch we have fried beans and then for supper we have beans and wild onions."

"We have a rule here" said Big Cat.

"Before we eat, we wash up"

"I washed my hands last night" said Boob.

"I'm not talking about hands, son, I mean you smell."

"I don't smell anything." answered Boob.

Let's go." said Big Cat.

"Where?" asked Elijah.

"Down at the creek of course"

"I can't wash with them" said Sidney.

"We already got that figured out" said Shoeless.

"Follow me" said Big Cat.

The four got in line and followed Big Cat

25

and Shoeless to the creek. When they arrived
Big Cat said

"You boys go over there by that tree
stump, take off your clothes and jump in."

"Here's some soap" Shoeless threw at
them. Elijah fell in trying to catch it. Big Cat
and Shoeless then walked up the creek about
100 feet. He and Big Cat strung some canvas
they had brought with them across the creek.

On each side of the bank were thick
bushes so Sidney could get behind the canvas
and not be seen. Shoeless threw her a bar of
soap too.

"I'll be sitting up here on the little hill, no
one will bother you" said Shoeless.

"What about our canvas?" asked Boob?

"Sorry boys, ladies first" replied
Shoeless. With that the boys took off their
clothes and threw them on the bank.

"No you don't" shouted Shoeless.

"Put them clothes in a neat pile"

The boys put their clothes in orderly,
neat groups.

"For a minute there I thought I was back
at the orphanage" said Aubrey.

The boys stood their naked looking at
the water.

"Best thing to do is jump in all at once,"
said Shoeless.

With that the boys jumped in.

"AAuuuggghhhh!" they all shouted.
They water was cold. It was so cold even

penguins would not get in.

The boys were fighting for the soap; for they knew the sooner you washed the sooner you could get out.

Up the creek they heard another shout. Sidney had jumped in.

Soon all were through.

They were dressed again but were shivering and shaking. They walked back up to the campsite and got in front of the fire. They got some hot beans and began to eat. The men knew they would without complaining. When you are hungry even beans look good. The hot food inside their bodies would warm them up.

.After they had eaten, they went down to the creek to wash the plates. Big Cat told them to go out gather some wood. They needed wood but more then that moving around would warm them up.

They could see several groups of men at different tents in the Hobo camp.

Later, waiting for lunch, while sitting around the fire some of the other Hobos came to the fire. One was short with a derby on, overalls with tools sticking out of the pockets. Another was tall, rail thin, and had on a hat that looked like the one that President Lincoln wore. The other was about twenty-five, neat and clean. They stopped and looked at the children.

"Howdy, Tin Cup, see you got some

visitors."

"Yes, Big Cat came with them last night."

"Why don't you introduce us to them?"

"Of course where are my manners" said Tin Cup.

He pointed to the short one,

"This is, Tool Man and the tall one there is Preacher and Just Sam."

He then pointed from left to right at the children.

"That is Boob, Aubrey, Elijah and Sidney"

"Nice to meet you boys and you too young lady" said the Preacher.

"Grab a log and sit down fellows" said Tin Cup.

"What you cooking?" asked the Preacher.

"Beans!" the children shouted all at once.

The men laughed.

"Tin Cup, I swear when you die they're going to put hot sauce with beans in your body instead of embalming fluid." said the Preacher.

"I thought it was the fire that made it so hot" said Aubrey.

"Tin Cup loves hot sauce, sometimes he even puts it in his water." said the Preacher.

"I just like the stuff" replied Tin Cup.

In the next few minutes the story of the children's plight was told to them.

Big Cat and the men walked away from the fire. They stood there talking for a few minutes. The men then left and Big Cat came back.

"They're not going to turn us in, are they?" asked Boob.

"Don't know" said Tin Cup.

Thirty minutes later the men came back. They were carrying some sacks with them. They sat down in front again and reached into the bags.

"We have been saving this, but we want the children to have it" said the Preacher.

In one bag he pulled out some potatoes, some salted bacon, and in another he pulled out some cans of corn.

Tin Cup knew that this was these men supply of food, yet they were willing to give it to the children.

"I tell you what, stay here and we all will have a feast tonight" said Tin Cup.

The men looked at each other and agreed.

That was a special night in Hobo camp.

By then all the Hobos had heard the children's story. Being good men in hard times, some missing their own families, they came bringing this and that, whatever they could spare. Some just came to be with the group and enjoy the laughter of the children. These men were not turned away because they had nothing to add to the meal, no, this was the true spirit of the camp, one for all and all for one.

But there are always exceptions, and it was coming this way.

"Well, look what we have here" said Bounty Man standing, looking down on the group.

All went silent.

"Looks like I found my little friends" he sneered.

"What happened to you?" asked Just Sam.

Bounty Man had scratches all over him, on his face, neck and hands.

"Nothing"

"Nothing, looks like a mountain lion got hold of you" said Just Sam.

"I said nothing" he snorted.

The group started laughing because they had heard the story. And no one liked him. Bounty Man turned red faced and stomped away.

"Better watch out for him" said Preacher Man.

"I don't trust that man, he's sure to come back for the children"

With that remark the children went silent and you could see the fear on their faces.

"Don't worry, nothing will happen to you here" said Just Sam.

"That's right" responded the rest of the men.

The tension faded and the party began again. It was good for the children and especially good for the men. It almost made them believe that hope would win and they too would one day be with their families. But until then, these children were their adopted family and nothing was going to happen to them. In fact from that point on the word was passed from Hobo camp to Hobo camp to watch out for these children and take care of them.

The following night they had to go, it was time. But the men noticed that Bounty Man was packing his stuff too. They knew him too well; he was waiting to get Big Cat and the children alone and then take them and turn them in.

That was not going to happen if the men in the camp had anything to do with it. They came up with a plan and whiskey was the answer. If there was one thing Bounty Man like more than money it was whiskey.

The men decided to have a drinking party. They knew that Bounty Man would invite himself to the party. In fact they were counting on it.

At dark the party began. They were sure to raise enough noise to attract his attention. It worked.

"Here he comes" said Tin Cup.

"Hey fellows" said Bounty Man sitting down with the group around the camp fire.

The men had a special drink for him.

They had put a bottle aside with something extra in it and only let him drink from it. In it was something to make him fall asleep.

"What's the occasion boys?"

"Tin Cup had forgotten he had some bottles stashed away, so he gave us some" said Just Sam.

The men drank out of the good bottle and pretended to be drunk. After an hour Bounty Man was done, he was out cold.

"OK boys, let's go" said the Preacher.

They picked him up, one on each leg and arm and one holding the head. They carried him to a wheel barrel, put him in and rolled him to the sidetrack past the town. It took all their strength to lift him into the boxcar. Just Sam threw in his pack and belongings.

"Think that stuff will keep him out?" asked Tool Man.

"An elephant wouldn't wake up for at least two days" replied Just Sam.

"Is this the right train" asked Just Sam.

"This is the one, don't worry" said the Preacher.

Since Bounty Mans train left before the train that was to take the children and headed in another direction there wasn't anyway Bounty Man would find them.

It was now dark, time for them to leave.

They had to go to the other side of town where, the thumpers wouldn't see them.

The engine had already joined up with

the boxcars and was starting to pull the line.

Big Cat put the children into the car and then jumped up himself.

A strange sight it was, in a lonely spot on a lonely line there was a group of men, poor all, some in ragged clothes, who had given, for some, their last bit of food to the children.

They had taken the danger away from them.

Now they were saying goodbye.

"Here, have some water" said Tin Cup with a canteen in his hand.

"Nooo" the children said all at once.

"You take care of them children, Big Cat!" yelled one.

"You young'uns do what Big Cat tells you to do, you hear!" yelled another.

Some lifted their arms to wave goodbye.

Some just looked, hating for them to leave. For just a little bit, for a little time they had forgotten their plight, to enjoy the innocence of children.

The steam engine was getting louder pulling on the line, the boxcar started moving.

The children were standing up in the doorway, all waving to the men. If you looked through the smoke from the engine you could see some young and old forgotten men, some supposing to be hard and cold, with a tear coming down their face.

Bounty Man had awakened up in jail. He had a headache like no other that he ever had before. He thought the thumpers must have raided the camp. But where were the other men who had been at that drinking party. His head hurt too much to think on it too long.

A guard came up to the jail cell door.

"Alright, my darling, time to shower and put on clean clothes, in an hour you'll be going before the judge" the guard said in a thick Irish brogue.

"Not another Irish" said Bounty Man

"Who let you in down here, I haven't seen you before" asked the Bounty Man.

"Oh, you don't like the Irish, do you?" said Tom O'Brian.

"Go to…. Ow" said Bounty Man.

Before he could finish the guard hit him over the head with a Billy Club.

"What you do that for?" asked Bounty Man.

"We don't have that kind of language here" said Sean.

What in the world was going on, he had never seen this guard or this jail before. Later he changed into prison black and white suit and brought before the judge.

The judge was His honor Michael O'Brian, from the old country. Yes, the father of guard Sean O'Brian.

As Bounty Man stood in front of the judge he heard the clerk of court say.

"Your honor, Mr. Silas Brown here (his real name) is charged with sneaking on a railroad car with the intent of not paying for the legal fare. He's also charged with being a vagrant; he has no job or way to pay for the fare"

"May, I say something, your esteem" said Sean.

"Yes you may" said the judge.

"This man seems to regard the Irish as some lowly miscreant"

"Oh he does, does he" said the judge.

"I never called him no such name, I just said he should sweep the floors with the rest of his kind" blurted out Bounty Man.

Wrong thing to say. The People in the court room gasped.

"Do you know where you are?" asked the judge.

"Sure I know I'm in Hazeltown, Georgia" said Bounty Man with confidence.

"You're where?" again asked the judge.

"I'm in Hazeltown, Georgia"

"Son, you are in Chicago" said the judge.

"What you trying to pull, I'm in Hazeltown" said Bounty Man.

"No, you are in Chicago" repeated the judge.

"What makes you think you are in Georgia" asked the judge.

"Because that's where I am, dam... it!" shouted Bounty Man.

"We will not have that language in my

courtroom, now one last time, where are you?"

"I told you, you stupid Irish, I'm in Georgia!" shouted Bounty Man.

That did it. The judge sentenced him to six months in the Bear Rabbit Asylum for the mentally ill. Bounty Man screamed all the way out of the courtroom, still believing he was in Georgia. It took him two months to be convinced he really was in Chicago. They never saw him again in the Hobo camp. Word was passed down through other travelers of the line that he had quit drinking and was working at the beef yard in Chicago.

He never did figure out how he got to Chicago.

CHAPTER FOUR

They traveled all night; the next stop wasn't till Pulliam Hill, North Carolina. The train traveled into the mountains, where there were no Thumpers. They tended to stay around the towns, where they could get good food, and wait for the next train to come into town. They didn't have any reason to go further up in the mountains where walking and getting a good place to stay was hard. So Big Cat and his merry band could settle down and enjoy the scenery as it passed by. But the strangest thing began to happen. Every so often a single man or a group of Hobo's would appear out of the woods and wait by the track. They had canvas bags, canteens by their sides. On one occasion all the children were on the floor looking out. Big Cat was standing by the boxcar door.

"Look there!" Sidney pointed to a man beside the tracks.

They all looked toward the front of the train. Standing there was a Hobo wearing an old floppy hat, he had a grey beard and wore run down clothes. He had a sack in his hand. He was looking for the boxcar they were in. As the car came by he swung the bag into the car, smiled and waved. He then turned around and disappeared into the woods. Sidney had to jump out of the way to keep the bag from hitting her. Boob went over to the bag and opened it up. Inside were some cans, beans, corn and some tins of sardines. Also was a canteen of good cold mountain water. They found a note that read.

"We will be watching for you, let you know what's up ahead. Good luck to the children" sighed Old Ben. It happened again and again all along the track. Big Cat got a lump in his throat, he knew how hard life was for these men and yet they gave all they could, for the children. From this point on Big Cat would not let anyone talk ill of the Hobo's. That night the merry band feasted on vegetables and sardines. The train was slowing down for a bend in the track as it climbed higher and higher up the mountains. Two men ran out of the woods and jumped onto the boxcar. It happened so quick that Sidney yelled. Big Cat turned from what he was doing to get ready to fight, if needed. It wasn't needed; both of the men wore old army jackets and World War One campaign hats. You know the hats with the pointed tops. One of them spoke up,

"Sorry about scaring you, but we had to run hard to get aboard"

We heard Big Cat was in need of sleep"

So we will watch while you get some sleep."

"How in the world did you know that?" asked Sidney.

"The Green Eyed Owl told us" said the other man.

"The Green Eyed Owl?" said the children all at once.

"You mean you never heard of the green eyed owl?"

"No" all the children answered.

Big Cat smiled. Hobo's have a way of telling stories when they didn't want you to know the truth.

"Sit down and I'll tell you the story"

The children sat down eagerly.

"It was a long time ago, when there wasn't many who lived in this area. There was a women who some thought was a witch. She had a place of her own up near the Black Woods, North Carolina; it's now called Bear Holler."

The children looked at each other when that name came up.

"She was living there with her animals, when some men came into the area. These were very bad men, robbers and highway men all. When they came upon a homestead they raided it, took their goods and left. That is until they came upon the witch. The animals had warned her that they were coming. She had a plan, a plan that would forever change their lives. The men were riding up on horse back when suddenly the horses stopped. They would not go up to the house. I'll tell you how I heard it."

He continued

"There were three of them. One was

thin with a big bushy beard. His face didn't look right, you looked at him from the front and it seemed that while his eyes were looking at you his mouth and chin was ajar to one side. The reason for this was years earlier it had been broken in a fight and was never fixed. That's why he was so thin; he only ate food that was boiled. The other man was heavyset; he too had a bushy beard. He had hard cold back eyes. The third was a young boy. But don't let this fool you; he had done his share of evil. His hair was long and was almost grey. This boy had seen a lot of hard living for that to happen. All of them had long rifles."

"Grat, what is wrong with these horses?" asked the heavyset man to the thin one.

"Dang, if I know" answered Ug. He was called this because of his jaw. No matter how hard they tried the horses would not move."

"Don't look like no one's here" said the boy.

"Go see, we'll keep you covered" said Grat.

The boy got off his horse, took his rifle and started toward the cabin. When he got to the porch he raised it and went in. It was empty. He went back outside and spoke,

"No one here, come on" said the boy.

Still the horses would not move. The men got off and went to the cabin. When they walked inside they weren't sure just what lived here. There was a big black kettle boiling in the fire place, all kinds of plants and herbs were lying around on tables. There were jars of bats, of dried fish, chicken bones and bird feathers. Even though the fire was burning it was cold inside.

"Someone was here the pot is still boiling" said Grat.

"Don't matter, let's eat and take what we want" said the boy.

Grat walked over to the kettle found a spoon beside it and dipped it in. When he pulled it out, he jumped back and dropped the spoon.

"AAuuuuggghhh!" he screamed

Both Ug and the boy turned from looking to see what they could steal and looked at him.

"What's the matter?" asked the boy

"There's, there's, there's eyes in it" Grat said.

"Eyes?" the others said at the same time.

"Yea, eyes"

The pot was full of eyes, lizards' eyes, bird eyes. They didn't know but it was a special brew, needed for curing some sick animals."

"I'm not eating this"

"I don't like this place" mumbled Ug.

"There's nothing here to steal" said the boy.

"Let's get out of here" said Grat.

They walked to the door and opened it,

and they stood still. Outside was the thickest fog you had ever seen. You couldn't see anything pass the porch. For a minute they stood there looking out, not believing what they saw. Grat moved first. They moved around in the fog, not seeing anything. Moving away from each other until the boy was by himself.

"Do you see the horses?" asked the boy.

No answer.

"Do you see the horses?" he asked again.

No answer again.

The boy was getting scared now, and it took a lot to get him scared.

"Grat?"

"Where are you?"

"They are gone" said a women's voice from behind him.

"What the..." the boy said as he turned around.

Out of the fog came the form of a lady, with a long brown dress on. She walked towards him.

"What do you mean, they are gone?" he asked.

"They are no more, they have gone to where they will do no more harm" she said.

"Look, I'm not going to ask you..."

She raised her hand. He stopped talking as if on command.

"I have spared you; from now on you will

not hurt People, and steal from them. From this moment on you will protect the poor, the innocent. It will be your job to warn them of danger." she said.

"Look, you'll crazy" he said as he turned around and walked into the fog.

A few minutes later the sound of the Eastern Screech Owl could be heard. It is said she turned him into this. From now on when you heard a Screech Owl, beware, especially the green eyed one, he's warning you of danger.

"That's why when you see the green eyed owl you know it's the boy, for his eyes are green and his feathers are grey" said one of the men to the children.

The children didn't say anything, first they had to shut their mouths.

"Better get some sleep." said Big Cat. "

Big Cat and the children lay down and were soon fast asleep. The two men stood guard over them the rest of the night, and every once in a while you could hear the Screech Owl in the distance.

The sun was rising, the birds were waking up. The two men were standing by the open door.

"Time for us to go, Dead Horse Turn is coming up"

"Dead Horse Turn?" asked Sidney.

"Everything in these mountains is named for a place, a person or story" said one of the men.

"Dead Horse Turn was named for a train accident during the Civil War. The Yankees were sending fresh horses to the troops in Georgia. The confederates heard about it and sabotaged the rails. So when the train hit this area, the train derailed and a lot of horses were killed. After that the name stuck."

"We are leaving at Dead Horse, best of luck to you"

"Thanks for helping" said Big Cat

"No problem, once we found out it was you and the children we had to help"

The train slowed down at Dead Horse Turn, and the men jumped off and went into the woods. Just past the turn they saw two men standing by the rails, these men were not Hobo's. Big Cat was worried they might be Thumpers. But, when he got a better look he saw that they were local farmers. They had a bag in each hand. When the boxcar came by they swung the sacks into the car, waved and left.

"This is really getting strange" said Big Cat.

"What is?" asked Boob.

"I've never seen this before, it's like someone is looking down on you children, now the farmers are helping" he said.

Aubrey opened the sacks. One had some cured ham, made on a local farm. The other had some clothes in it. They had overalls

44

of all sizes; all the children had at least one size that fit them.
"Save the ones that fit, later we will find a place to bathe and then put them on" said Big Cat.

CHAPTER FIVE

"It's not far to Table Rock, we have to get off there" said Big Cat.

"Pack the stuff up and be ready to jump" he said

"Oh, no" answered Elijah.

They waited thirty minutes.

"It's time" said Big Cat.

He had them lined up by the door ready to go. Each one carried a sleeping bag with their utensils inside along with some clothes.

"This time, hold you sleeping bag close to you, that way when you land it will soften the blow" said Big Cat.

"Go, Go, Go!" shouted Big Cat

All got up enough nerve and jumped. The bags did help, except for Elijah, when he hit the ground the bag bounce with him and they flew into the air. He bounced down a hill and wasn't seen anymore. When the rest of them got to their feet, Sidney said,

"Where's Elijah?"

"Last I saw of him he was bouncing that way" pointed Boob.

They picked up the stuff and headed down the grassy hill next to the wood line. When they got to the bottom, they stopped, looking at a man holding Elijah.

"I was walking up to meet you when this young fella flew into my arms" he laughed.

He let Elijah go, who immediately turned

46

red in the face.

"We heard this is where you would get off, Big Cat" said the stranger

"You leaving now?" he asked.

"Yep" said Big Cat.

Sidney walked up beside Big Cat and touched the edge of his pants leg and looked up.

The other children had a lost look also.

Big Cat cleared his throat and said,

"Maybe I can go a little farther, won't hurt none."

The children smiled and Sidney hugged his waist.

"None of that, you know I can't stay forever"

"I'm called Sooner" said the stranger.

"Follow me"

Boob started to open his mouth when Sidney said,

"Don't Ask"

He led them through the woods across some plowed fields up to a cabin that was sitting on the side of a hill. It was a big cabin, forty feet by sixty feet, with a wooden porch in front. On that porch was a lady in a light blue dress. She and her husband looked to be about sixty years old. It was hard to tell in the mountains, the life was hard and life took a toll on a person's health and looks.

"Bring them on up here, Sooner" she yelled across the field.

They walked up to the porch and stopped.

"My, my, you sure do need a bath bad.

They did, their face and bodies were covered by the smoke from the steam engine.

"And you too" she pointed at Big Cat.

"Yess'um" he said.

"Sooner, take that man to the creek, give him some fresh clothes, I'll wash his and the children's clothes tomorrow." she ordered.

"You" she said pointing a finger at Big Cat."

"Ma am" Big Cat answered.

"Call me Big Cat."

"You still have to take a bath, Mr. Cat" she said

"Yes'um"

"You children, follow me"

"Yes'um" they said.

Once inside she gave orders like a drill sergeant.

"You boys go onto the back porch and wait; I'll be there in a minute"

"Yes'um"

"Now, young lady, come with me to the kitchen, I have a hot tub of water waiting for you."

"Yes'um"

She took Sidney into the kitchen, shut the door and window. She told Sidney to get undressed and get in the tub. She gave her a bar of soap and a rag.

"Start washing"

"Yes um"

"I'll be back in a minute" she said. She went out the kitchen door and headed to the back porch.

"What are you waiting for, an invitation"

"No ma'mam" they all said.

"One of you get undressed and the others go get water to put in the pot on the fire"

"There's a pump over by the fence"

The boys looked and in the back yard was a fire with a big pot over it, boiling water.

"Put the hot water into this tub and go do the same thing until all of you are clean."

"And don't use the same water for two, I can spot a dirt line on you fifty yards away" she said.

"Yes'um"

With that she went back to Sidney

"You are looking better, let's wash that hair. I have some soap mixed with some honey and some herbs that will clean your hair and make it soft and smell good too."

Sidney finished bathing and she did feel a whole lot better.

"Leave you clothes there on the chair, I'll wash them tomorrow."

Sidney started to reach for her extra overalls when, "No, honey" The old lady said.

"Put this on"

The old lady took a small blue dress from the hook in the side room.

It used to belong to my daughter. I think it will fit you.

"I haven't had a dress on in a long time" said Sidney

"Go ahead, please"

"Alright"

Sidney put the dress on and the old women combed her hair and even put a bow in it. She didn't have any shoes to fit, and the shoes she had didn't look right so she went barefooted. The dress came down to her ankles, so you couldn't tell too much.

"I'm so tired of toting water" said Aubrey.

"Boob is the last one" said Elijah.

"Hurry Up, my waters getting cold" yelled Boob.

"I'll get cold him" said Aubrey.

"Wait, do this" said Elijah.

"Do what?" asked Aubrey.

Elijah pointed to an ant bed near a fence nearby.

"Come on, I'm getting cold" shouted Boob.

"We're coming boss, we're coming" they said

They boys put the ants in water, but not hot, hot water would kill them. The walked over to the tub and poured the bucket behind Boob where he wouldn't see them.

"That's cold, go heat up some more" yelled Boob.

"Yes, boss" they said.

50

The boys stood by the pot and fire and waited.

Boob noticed them standing there.

"Hey, what's wrong with you, what are you staring at?" asked Boob.

"We're waiting for you to get the feeling, you know like at church" said Aubrey.

"You're crazy" said Boob.

Just then the ants found out they didn't like water and started to crawl all over Boob, some biting. Boob jumped up out of that tub, landed with his feet on the porch yelling and dancing.

"Look at him go" said Elijah.

"I'll say that boy sure has got the feeling, don't you?" said Aubrey.

They both began to laugh and the more they watched Boob jumping up and down, the harder it got.

Down at the creek,

"Big Cat, what are you going to do with the young'uns?" asked Sooner.

"I don't know" he replied.

"You know there isn't any treasure on that mountain." said Sooner.

"I know there's nothing to it, but it's a dream, they have had so little, maybe for a short time they can have hope. That's not so bad, is it?" said Big Cat.

"No, maybe not, just be careful, there are strange things that happen on that mountain." Sooner said.

"Like what?" asked Big Cat.

"You'll see, anyway come on, the misses probably has supper on."

Sooner, Big Cat, Aubrey, Elijah and Boob, who was squirming, were sitting at the table. The door to the back room opened and in walked the lady with someone the fellas hadn't seen before. All stared. There stood Sidney in her dress, her hair made up and shinning, looking at them. She was starting to turn red in the face.

Big Cat stood up.

"Up boys" he said.

"Why?" asked Boob

"Now" he repeated.

The boys stood up.

"Because a lady just entered the room" said Big Cat.

Big Cat walked around the table and pulled Sidney's chair out for her to sit down. Sidney walked forward and sat down, still blushing. When they were all seated they said a prayer. Sooner started.

"Lord, bless this house, bless our friends, bless the fields, bless the pigs, bless the good weather, bless our neighbors, bless our food, bless the flowers, bless the bees, bless the."

The boys looked up at one another.

"Bless the new crop, bless the chickens, bless my dogs, and bless the cow"

"Sooner!" said the old lady.

52

"Amen" he finished.

They started eating and it was some good old country cooking. Cooked ham, tomato's, and beans with fresh bread and butter.

"You look mighty pretty, Sidney" said Big Cat.

"Thank you" she said in a low voice.

"I almost forgot you were a girl" said Boob.

"Why can't you sit still" asked Big Cat to Boob.

"He's seen the Lord" said Aubrey.

The rest looked at Boob.

"I got some lotion for that" said the lady.

"Thanks" said Boob, for he needed some relief, bad.

When the meal was over, Sidney helped pick up the dishes.

"You don't have to do that" said the old lady.

"No, I want to"

"It's been a while since I had a girl help me around the house" she said.

"Where is your girl?" asked Sidney.

The old lady went quiet.

"She's left us, she died with the influenza of 1918, and she was about your age"

"I'm sorry" said Sidney feeling bad about bringing it up.

"No, she was with us for a while and the

53

Lord decided to take her, he had a reason"

"Let's do the dishes and I'll show you how to make bread for the morning" smiled the old lady

"Ok"

While the women were busy in the kitchen, the boys went outside with the men. The men sat in rocking chairs on the porch. The boys went into the yard to roam around as boys will do.

"That lotion really worked" said Boob.

Just then they heard a loud grizzly scream from high on the mountain. It echoed on down through the valley and bounced off the sides of the cabin. The boys froze and then ran to the porch.

"What was that?" they asked Sooner.

"That's why they call it Bear Holler Mountain" he said

"You mean the bears are doing that?" asked Aubrey.

"We really don't know, but the tale is that they are"

"Why?"

"There's a story the Cherokee Indians used to tell, about a beautiful bear a long time ago, she was the leader of her clan. When the white men came into the mountains they took her cubs and she tried to defend them, she was killed. The men took the cubs away. From that day on she's still searching for them. That's why when you hear that scream it's her

54

calling out for them"

"It's an old Indian tale."

"But the sound" said Aubrey.

"Your never know, the mountains are full of mystery." answered Sooner.

The boys stayed on the porch with the men until it was time to go in. The old women came out of the kitchen when she heard them come in she said,

"Sooner, show the boys were to sleep upstairs, I and Sidney will sleep in our bed; you and Mr. Cat make pallets on the floor here."

"No problem, Martha" said Sooner.

"Martha that was nice for what you did for Sidney." said Big Cat.

"Little girls are special, they need to dress up once in a while" she said.

Big Cat walked into the kitchen with Martha while Sooner took the boys upstairs. Sidney was standing there with flower on her hands and face. Her hair was protected by a bandana that Martha had tied around her head.

Sidney looked up and grinned.

"I've made bread" she beamed.

"My, you are growing up" said Big Cat.

"I'm proud of you"

Sidney had never had a father, never had anyone tell her that they were proud of her.

It made her feel good inside.

"Let's clean up now, leave the bread to rise overnight and first thing in the morning I'll teach you how to bake It." said Martha.

Sidney covered the dough with some cloth and both she and Martha washed up in the sink using a hand pump.

"See you in the morning, we're going to bed, us women have to get up early" Martha said.

Sidney beamed again, she was called a women. She marched proudly to the bedroom with Martha by her side. She was holding Marta's hand and she couldn't resist looking back at Big Cat and smile.

The boys were upstairs in the loft. There was a big old bed and all three of them fit comfortably. It had one window that looked out on the front of the house. The moon was up and shinning in on their faces. They had the cover pulled up to their necks. That grizzly sound came again. The boys pulled the cover over their heads.

The next day the women were up early, they had baked the bread, cooked some eggs and bacon.

When they were through it was time to wake the boys up.

The men were already up and outside chopping wood.

"Sidney go upstairs and wake them lazy boys up" said Martha.

"Here take this, this will get them up" said Martha handing Sidney the cornstalk broom.

"Yes ma'am"

Sidney went upstairs and opened the door. At first she didn't see them. They were covered up by the bedspread.

"OK, get up, time to eat" she yelled.

They didn't move.

"I said get up!"

Downstairs Martha grinned.

"Go away" said Boob.

"Yea, get out of here" said Elijah They covered their heads up again. With that Sidney took the cover and yanked it off the bed.

"Stop!" Stop!" screamed Boob.

Sidney didn't answer; she took that broom and began to wail at the bed.

Those boys were jumping and hollowing all over the place. It didn't take long before they were standing by the bed.

"You got five minutes to get dressed and come down, if you don't I'll be back" She then turned around and left. They didn't see the simile on her face.

The boys just stared. Something had come over Sidney. She was no longer the old Sidney, something had changed in her.

The men had washed up and were sitting at the table when the boys came down. Martha and Sidney were going back and forth from the kitchen with plates of food. They sat down.

"Say the prayer" said Martha.

The boys looked over at Sooner, waiting

for it to come. Then he started.

"Bless this house, bless our friends, bless our fields, bless the pigs, bless good weather, bless our food, bless our flowers, bless the bees, bless the chickens, bless my dogs, bless the co."

"Sooner" said Martha loudly.

"Amen" said Sooner.

"This is mighty good bread" said Sooner.

"You can thank Sidney for that, she made it" said Martha.

"It is good" said Big Cat.

"You boys think so?" asked Big Cat

All at once they answered,

"This is good bread, Sidney, thank you."

When the breakfast was through Sooner said,

"Ok, boys, outside, time to milk the cow."

Now the boys really did look at each other. Sidney smiled.

The boys went outside with Sooner and Big Cat

"Grab that bucket and bring it over here" said Sooner to the boys.

Boob went to get it, thinking he would give it to Elijah or Aubrey there by getting him out of this. He went to hand it to Aubrey when Sooner said,

"Sit on this stool and get under her."

"Now grab each tit and pull down, milk

will come out"

Boob did as he was instructed, but no milk came out.

"Pull down harder" He did and milk began to flow.

"Now take turns" said Sooner

Boob did fifteen minutes and Elijah and Aubrey did their fifteen minutes, soon the bucket was half full.

"You can stop now; don't want to drain her dry"

"Aubrey, take the bucket into the house for Martha"

Aubrey grabbed the bucket and went into the house.

Elijah went in with him.

"I have an idea"

"What" asked Aubrey?

Elijah whispered in his ear.

"Ok"

They went back outside where Boob was standing by the cow.

"Hey, Boob, I bet you can't ride her" said Elijah.

"Sure I can"

"You can't"

"I can too"

"Show me then, bigmouth" said Elijah.

With that Boob got a wooden crate and put it by the cow and got on. That cow was not used to anyone or anything sitting on its back. It started running around and around with Boob hanging on for dear life.

"Ride'em cowboy" yelled Elijah.

"What in the world?"

Martha said while looking out the kitchen window, watching the cow run with Boob screaming on his back. That cow took Boob for a ride, around the back of the house, around the front of the house and headed to the creek in the back. Only one problem with that, Mary the cow had no intentions of getting wet. Right before the creek she stopped. Boob didn't, he flew off that cow and landed butt first in the creek. The men walked over to him, to see if he was alright. When they found out he was, Big Cat said,

"Taking your bath a little early aren't you?"

Boob didn't say anything. He was still sitting there when the men were walking back to the house. They were trying not to laugh out loud.

CHAPTER SIX

Today was the day they had to leave.

They were sitting down for breakfast that Sidney helped to prepare. She was getting to be a good little housekeeper.

"Say the prayer" said Martha.

The boys started giggling; they knew what was coming, again. Sooner started,

"Bless this house, bless our friends, bless the fields, bless the pigs, bless the food, bless the flowers, bless the bees, bless my dogs, and bless the cow.

"Sooner!" said Martha.

"Amen" said Sooner.

They had all their stuff packed and ready to go. Martha had told Sidney, and the boys, to stop by on their way back. The cow, well, the cow was kind of skittish. Off they went down the road with Sooner and Martha waving from the porch. In the mountains there are homes like this almost everywhere, where People welcome you to their house, will share their food and lodging with you. These are families of the earth, seen hard times, hard living, but love never abandons them.

The little band headed up the trail to the mountain, Big Cat had decided that he could spare some more time and take the children up there. They walked down tree shaded trails, up and over fallen tree logs, across streams. It was twilight; they had to find a place to stop for the night. Big Cat found a good spot next to a fresh water stream. The boys went out to get some limbs and twigs to use for a fire. Big Cat and Sidney were getting the pots out of the sack and preparing some food. Soon all were around the fire and eating to their hearts content.

"Show me that map Boob" said Big Cat.

Boob dug in his pack and took out the map and handed it to Big Cat. He turned it facing the fire so he could see it better

"It's an old map alright, might be something to this."

He studied it for a while and then said,

"As best as I can make out we are about two miles from this valley." He pointed to on the map.

"It has an X here, but it really doesn't say where, it's going to take some hunting."

"You think we can find it?" asked Aubrey.

"Might be a fifty-fifty chance, who knows, we'll give it a try"

"Let's get some sleep and get started in the morning"

The glow from the fire showed five sleeping bags around it. The only sound was the popping from the wood on the fire.

They had been asleep for a while when the scream of the bear came from on top of the mountain. The boys pulled their bags next to each other. Sidney pulled hers next to Big

Cat's.

Big Cat smiled and went back to sleep.

The next morning found them going higher and higher up the mountain. Soon they found that they were lost. They have never been here before and the map was not one for details, such as terrain.

They were sitting in a little clearing with brush and tall trees all around eating a cold noon meal

Big Cat was worried; he had the children to worry about. What he had gotten them into.

Boob looked up, stared and rubbed his eyes, he wasn't sure he was seeing what he thought he was seeing. The rest noticed that Boob was staring with his mouth open. They looked around and all saw six men, little men, dressed like the Robin Hood gang, with green clothes and little green hats.

One walked forward and said.

"Come with us, we were looking for you"

"You knew we were coming?" asked Big Cat.

"We know all that moves on the mountain"

"Come" he said again.

"Who are you?" asked Big Cat.

"The Lady of the Forrest will tell you, come, please, no harm will come to you"

"Children, let's go"

As they walked behind this strange group of men, Big Cat was wondering who this

Lady of the Forrest was.

The group had walked about a mile up the mountain when they came to a clearing, a beautiful clearing. It had a grassy area in front that led to a one story rock house with flowers planted in front. The door was one that was split in two, a Dutch door, where you could keep the bottom shut and the top open.

Standing in front of it was a young woman who was dressed in a long brown dress; she had brown hair to her shoulders and dark brown eyes. She had her hand up to her eyes to shield from the sun so she could see them.

When they reached to where she was standing the men went off to a little rock house that was on the right side of the big one.

"Welcome, come inside, supper is on the table."

"Thank you" replied Big Cat.

They were led inside and it was cool, a refreshing cool.

"Wash up over there, she pointed to the sink"

"Put your things over there, she pointed to a place by the door."

When they were settled down at the table, she served vegetables, no meat of any kind.

"I hope you don't mind, we don't eat meat here, no animals are killed here." she said.

"Don't mind at all" answered Big Cat.

The meal was good and filling, the children ate plenty. The house was neat and there were flowers and herb plants and jars filled with herb seeds all around. The room was from one side of the house to the other. It had two fire places, one for the kitchen and the other on the opposite wall. In-between was some chairs and furniture. All hand make from the trees. At the rear of the house it looked like two bedrooms. It was a house where one had lived in for a long time.

"My name is Glenna" she said.

Big Cats family had come from the old country, so he knew that Glenna was Celtic for, from the valley or from the glen. The name fit her perfectly.

"I'm called Big Cat, this is Sidney, Boob, Aubrey and Elijah" said Big Cat.

"Big Cat?" she asked.

"Well, my legal name is James Dublin, but everyone calls me Big Cat" he smiled.

"James, that is a good name, I will call you James" she said.

And that was that, she said it in way that it wasn't asking, but in a way that was the way it was to be. The children grinned. Looks like Big Cat, Tom, had met his match.

"May I ask you a question?" said James to Glenna.

"Yes" she answered.

"Who are those little guys?"

"Those are the little People, surely you've heard of them"

"You trying to tell me they are leprechauns?"

"No" she laughed.

"They came here several years ago; they had been working for a circus. They were tired of People laughing and making fun of them. They came into the mountains and found me. We have been together ever since."

Later on after the meal he said,

"We must go now, can you show us the way to this spot" pointing to an area on the map.

"I don't know where you got this map, but you don't want to go there" she said.

"Why not?" he asked.

"It's on the far side of the mountain; it's the site of an ancient Indian burial mound. The X there on the map marks an cave that some say is haunted"

"I really don't know why, but I feel I must take the children there, something or someone has looked after them all the way here" James said

"I think they do have a Nahual over them, I sensed it when you came to the mountains" she said

"Nahual?" he asked.

"Yes, Aztec's believed in spirits that ruled the world, it's a type of guardian angel"

"I think maybe you are destined to go

there but remember an old Irish proverb.

"There are chests of gold within all the burial mounds, but mind the cats that guard them." she said.

"Please stay the night, it is getting dark, and it is not good to go walking on the mountain at night."

"Alright, thank you" James said

"Children, take your packs to the back room on the left, you can sleep there tonight" she said

The children were tired from the long walk here and they were fast asleep on two beds in the room. Sidney, of course, had one all to her self.

James was leaning against the porch column while Glenna was in a rocking chair near him. They both were looking out on the valley and listening to the night sounds.

"Why do you do this, bring the children here?" asked Glenna.

"I wasn't at first, I was just going to take them to Table Rock, but I have grown too fond of them, I must follow all the way now." he said.

"You have a good heart, James, but you are taking a chance" she answered.

"That place you want to go is sacred, it is protected by spirits, and only the chosen ones will be able to get there."

"You're talking about ghosts"

"There are some who think I am a witch because I live up here by myself"

"That was until the little People came, but not one has seen them"

"A witch?" he smiled.

"Yes, People who think just because you love nature and use its medicines, think you must be a witch"

"How long have you lived here?"

"My family has been here for generations, after my father and mother died, I stayed on. I probably will be the last"

"Why?"

"Who wants to marry a witch" she laughed

"Oh, I don't know, there might be someone" he answered.

They looked at each other for a second and then looked back out to the valley.

Unknown to them at the foot of the mountain were a group of men. These men were not here to be camping and enjoying the forest. They had heard of the children and the treasure map. These were hard men, not like the hobo's, who were placed in their predicament by the depression, but men who prayed on the innocent and poor to steal and kill to get what they wanted. And now they wanted the gold. It had to be gold, the gold of the Spanish soldiers from years ago. They were going to get it no matter what or who got in their way. They were seven of them, more than enough to handle four children and one man.

They had faced odds worse than that and succeeded. They were all sitting around a fire and talking. Jack was the leader; he was six feet tall, long hair and beard. He had done time for robbery and assault. Sam was five foot ten, long hair and mustache that came past his chin. He was mean, just mean; he was known to kick a dog just for looking at him. Picket, five foot eleven, bald and had the blackest eyes. He had escaped prison where he was serving time for murder. The rest, were Johnson, Pruittt, and Jamison.

They were followers.

All had weapons, some rifles, some pistols and all had a long knife, sometimes called an Arkansas toothpick.

"Do you really think that it's gold there're after?" asked Johnson.

"Sure, why else would a man go to all this trouble with a group of kids" answered Jack

"How much do you think there is?" asked Johnson again.

"Those Spanish knew how to find gold; it's more than enough for us. We could be rich for the rest of ours lives"

"How are we going to do this?"

"Try to remember. We are going to follow them and when they find the gold we jump them, got it?"

"Yea, sure" answered Johnson.

"Now get some sleep, we have to find

their trail in the morning" said Jack.

Each one went to sleep that night dreaming of how each one was going to spend that gold.

Early in the morning, before light, there came the scream of the bear. The men rose as one up from the ground.

"What was that?" asked Picket.

"Just a bear" said Jack.

"Never heard a bear sound like that" said Pruitt"

"That's because that's a spook bear" said Jamison.

"Spook bear?" said Pruitt.

"Everyone from these parts say a spook bear lives on the mountain." answered Jamison.

"Spook bear or no spook bear, lets get some sleep" ordered Jack. All laid back down, some stayed awake wondering about that bear.

The morning came clear and shinning through the leaves of the nearby trees. Tom and the children were ready to leave. The children were in the middle of the front yard while James and Glenna were standing on the porch.

"I know this is a wild goose chase, but I can't let the children go on alone, and they would." said Tom.

"They are determined" said Glenna.

"Be careful James, there are other men

on the mountain. Watch out for them." she said.

"Other men, how do you know?"

"The mountain told me."

"Be careful, and trust the signs" she continued.

"The signs?"

"You will know when you see them and trust in the children's Nahual"

When they had disappeared from sight, the little People came to Glenna's side.

"You want us to go with them?" asked one

"Yes, don't let them see you unless it's necessary."

"There are other men following them, be careful"

"We will, Glenna, don't worry"

With that the little People went back to their house to get their gear.

But Glenna was worried, something had come to the mountain and it was going to be a fight between good and evil. She wasn't sure who was going to win and she was frightened.

The morning was fresh but as the day wore on the heat of the day began to make the trip long and hard. They stopped in a little clearing to take a break.

"You sure we are going the right way" asked Boob.

"Glenna showed me the way on the map, it's not hard to find." said James.

71

"Can't wait to get the gold and get rich" said Aubrey.

"We don't know if there's any gold there or not" said James.

"Sure there is, the map says so." said Boob.

James didn't want to break their hearts so he remained quiet.

CHAPTER SEVEN

It was the next day when they came upon the site. There was a clearing in the forest. The trees seemed to open up to it. It was about the size of a baseball field. There were three mounds of dirt now covered with grass and forest leaves and twigs. These were the Indian burial mounds. In the middle were still the signs of a well worn path. At the end was the side of a rock face. The way the rocks were worn it looked like a skull.

All of them stopped when they saw this.

"I don't think I'm going any further" said Elijah.

"I'm not going in there" said Boob.

"Me neither" said Aubrey.

"Well, we are here now, it's getting late, let's make camp and we're check it out in the morning." said James.

"You mean we are staying here?" asked Elijah.

"This is what you came for" replied James.

"It's just a hole in the mountain" said Boob.

They made camp in the middle of the field. Soon it was dark and the glow of the firelight was the only light around. They all camped close to the fire as the light from it comforted them.

Out of the dark they heard the call of the

Screech Owl.

"What was that!" asked Elijah.

"That's the Screech Owl" said Sidney.

"Remember what the men said about that?" asked Aubrey

"Yea, when you hear the Screech Owl that means danger is near" said Sidney.

"We need to get some sleep" said James.

They got closer to the fire and in time each fell asleep. Not far down the mountain, the men of the other camp had heard the owl too.

"That's spooky" said Sam.

"It's just a hoot owl, you never heard a hoot owl before?" said Jack.

"Sure I have, it's just that one doesn't sound like any hoot owl I've ever heard."

"You'll forget all about that owl when we get that gold" said Jamison.

"What are we going to do with those kids and the man?" asked Sam.

"Dump them in that cave, no one will find them" said Jack.

The little men were nearby and they heard what the group was planning. Glenna wanted them to watch over the man and the children. Normally she didn't care what happened to strangers in her woods. But this little group of wayfarers was different. They had noticed her worry about the children. Glenna always looked after the children and animals. They also noticed that she was different around the man. Something was happening there and they were happy for her.

Even though she might not yet know it, but they knew her actions well, and they knew something was stirring there. They would do their best to help them.

The next morning was chilly, as mornings in the mountains tend to be. This morning there was a heavy fog in the forest from the ground to the tops of the trees. The little group of treasure hunters got their equipment packed and headed to the entrance of the cave.

The closer they got the slower they walked.

"Come on Boob" said Sidney.

Sidney was the only one who didn't seem afraid.

Maybe it was women feelings. That they get for knowing what is going to happen, before it happens.

Who knows, but she was steady as a rock.

"I'm coming" replied Boob.

The ground at the front of the cave was sand. It made no sound as you moved on it.

"I can't see" said Elijah.

"Wait, I'll light some matches" said James.

He lit a match and in doing so he found where long ago someone had left some torches. He lit one and it instantly caught and gave them some light. James found some more and lit them.

"Be careful, don't get them to close to you" he said.

The little group, each carrying a torch headed deeper into the cave.

Back at the other fire the men where standing around trying to get warm.

"Would you look at this fog" said Picket.

"It will burn off soon enough."

"It can't be much farther to go." said Jack.

"We will just follow this trail" said Jack.

The little men were not idle this morning. They had been working on that trail. They knew it split into two trails up the mountain. They covered the right one with sticks and leaves, while the rest were preparing the other for the men.

"This should slow them down a bit" said one of the little men.

"Hope so" said another.

They then left.

The men put out the fire and headed up the mountain. What they didn't know was that the trail they now followed would wind them around and around the mountain in circles.

They walked right past the trail the little men had covered up. In the distance the little men watched as the others took the bait.

"You sure we are going the right way?"

76

asked Sam.

"Why you asking?" said Jack.

"I haven't seen any footprints since we left" answered Sam.

"That don't mean anything, we're going up the mountain, isn't we."

Sam just looked at Jack hoping he was right.

The day had got longer and the sun hotter.

The men were walking slower along the trail.

One of them, Jamison, had fallen back behind the group. He wasn't used to all this walking, especially uphill. He had to stop now and then to get his breath. He stopped under a limb that was hanging over the trail. He took off his hat to wipe the sweat from his forehead. Out of the blue from that limb came an arm with a hand that had a club in it. It only took one tap and Jamison was down for the count

The little men came out from the bushes and tied him up. They tied a cloth over his mouth so he couldn't yell and warn the others.

They tied him to a long pole about ten feet long. It took two on each end of the pole to lift him and one to lead the way. They would switch off when one got tired.

When Jamison awoke all he saw was little men in green clothes carrying him god knows where. He tried to get loose but he was like a pig ready for roasting.

"No need to jerk around, you won't get away, besides we might drop you and that wouldn't feel good." said one.

"Mmmmmm....." replied Jamison.

His head still hurt.

"What did he say?" asked one of the little men.

"He said, Ok." one answered.

The others laughed all the way to slingshot.

They had been in the circus and knew how to make different equipment to show off their acrobatic skills.

One was being shot from a cannon and landing in a net. When they came to the mountain they kept up their skills by making them and placing them in different parts of the forest. It was for practice, they never knew they would need them for something else.

They came to the edge of a cliff about one hundred feet high and on the edge was build the largest slingshot the world had seen. It was made of a tall tree that was bent back almost to the ground without breaking. On it was a wood seat. When they got there the little men untied Jamison from the pole.

He was sitting on the ground watching the others bend back that tree. He had no idea what was coming next.

They took off the cloth around his mouth.

"What are you going to do?" he asked.

"We are going to teach you how to fly" said one.

"Fly?"

"But first you must understand, never come into these woods again. If you do you will never be seen again. You understand?"

Jamison was too scared. He was surrounded by ten little men in green clothes; all had knives on their sides.

"I understand"

"Load him up" shouted one.

"Nooo…oooo" shouted Jamison.

"Down there is a swamp, you will land safely. There is a trail that leads out of here, stay on it and you will come to an Inn. If you are still tied, they will help you. And don't come back." said the leader.

He was put on a forked limb. A kind of seat that was almost touching the ground. His hands were tied behind his back.

"Fire!" yelled the leader.

Swish went the tree, off flew Jamison up in the air, screaming all the way.

"Man look at him go!" shouted one of the little men.

He landed in a swampy area about five hundred feet from the mountain. He landed face down in the muck.

"He's needs more practice" said one laughing.

"That's one, come on we have more work to do" said the leader.

Jamison got up spitting mud and muck out of his mouth. He wasted no time in finding the trail and headed out of the forest.

"Let's take a break, Jack" said Sam.

"Alright, just for a few minutes"

"Where's is Jamison?" asked Pruitt.

"He chickened out" said Sam.

"That's Ok, more for us" answered Jack.

That was the kind of men they were, they didn't care for anyone but themselves. If one left they paid no attention to it.

Meanwhile back at the cave.

"This is bigger than I thought." said James.

"Looks like nothings here, let's go" said Boob.

"Not yet" answered James.

As they moved on into the cave the walls got further apart and the ceiling higher.

They Shadows were bouncing off the sides of the cave from the lights of the torches.

"The Shadows are doing funny things" said Sidney.

"You seen it too?" said Elijah.

"Seen what?" asked Aubrey.

"They are moving when we don't" she said.

"You heard of the Shadow People" said James.

"The Shadow People?" asked Boob.

"It started with the white People came to America and chased the Indians out of their homes and forests. Some say there are ghosts that stayed behind to protect their land. They usually only let you see them out of the corner of your eyes. But, sometimes when they have too, to protect or to warn, they will appear in front of you. People have said that they have red glowing eyes. Who knows, they might be here protecting something."

"We mean no harm, so I don't think we have anything to worry about."

Those that come here meaning to do harm, who knows." said Tom.

"Mr. Shadow man, I'm Boob and I don't mean any harm" said Boob.

"Me too, me too" said the other children.

James smiled. But then he thought,

"Me too" he said under his breath.

The men continued on they way to do harm. They didn't care who or what got in there way. They were going to get that gold. It was getting dark and the men decided to make camp for the night. It seemed they had been walking for miles and not getting anywhere.

"Man, I'm tired, you think we will find them tomorrow?" asked Sam.

"I've been thinking, we have walked all day and that mountain is always above us. Tomorrow we'll leave this path and head straight up It." said Jack.

The little men hiding in the woods didn't like that. The men were going to leave the false trail and head straight to the children.

"I have to go to the bathroom" said the man Johnson.

"What do you want us to do, hold your hand" said Picket. The men laughed.

Johnson went out into the dark, did his business, and was hitching up his pants when, you guessed it,

"Bonk!" on the head. The little men tied him to a pole and headed down to the flying machine.

"What's taking him so long, you think he got lost?" asked Sam.

"Who cares, let's get some sleep, he will be here in the morning.

All laid down and went fast to sleep, it had been a long hard day for them.

In the morning they awoke to find that Johnson was not there. They looked at each other.

"I've been thinking" said Sam.

"That could be dangerous." laughed Jack.

"No, I mean that's two of us that have disappeared since we've been on this mountain."

"They say this place is haunted."

"Johnson is just lost, it's easy to do on this mountain, now lets go" said Jack.

Johnson was sitting in the homemade chair on the tree. He was shaking so bad he almost fell out. He awoke and found himself sitting here surrounded by little men in green clothes.

He told himself if he ever lived though this he would never come back.

"You like to watch birds fly?" asked one of the little men

"What?"

"Do you like to watch birds flying?"

"Sure"

"Would you like to fly?"

"Guess so"

"Well, here's your chance"

"Fire!" yelled the little man in charge.

"He's going sideways" said one.

"He's going to hit that."

"Tree" finished the other man.

Sure enough Johnson hit a tree, bounced off and fell to the ground.

"You think he's alright?" asked one.

"Look!" said another pointing to Johnson

Johnson had gotten to his feet, when hitting the tree the rope that tied his hands came undone. He put both of his hands to his head and moaned. Then he walked off down the trail.

"He's Ok"

"Let's go"

"Two down, four to go" said the one of the Little Men.

Jamison had walked several miles to he came to a road. There he met a farmer pulling a wagon with a worn out horse. He was covered with swamp mud from head to toe.

"Whoa there May Bell" said the farmer to his horse.

"You alright, mister?" he asked.

Jamison just stared straight ahead.

The farmer got off his horse and helped him to the wagon.

"Come with me, Son" said the farmer.

Somehow he got Jamison in the wagon and drove on down the road. Jamison didn't say anything.

"There's an Inn down the road a piece, I'll take you there."

The Inn had been here at the fork of the Dead Mule Trail Road and the Sumter Mill Road since the founding of this area in 1804. It had been rebuilt several times. It was now a white two story stone building with a large front door. Above it was the name Jacobs Inn. Nobody remembered how it got that name. Now a husband and wife, Mr. Ralf and Sally Canton owned it.

Even though it was early in the morning there were several men already there. They came here to they sit and talk about the farms, animals, and other important things.

The door opened and in walked the farmer with Jamison.

"Found him on the road" said the farmer.

"Sit down here mister" said Mr. Canton. .

"Bring a touch of whiskey, Ma" said Mr. Canton to his wife.

By now some were standing or were seated at the table.

Jamison took the whisky, downed it, cleared his throat and spoke.

"Thanks"

"What happed?" asked one of the men.

"I was up on the mountain walking along and all of a sudden something hit me on the head. When I awoke I was tied to a pole and taken to a tree. These little men in green clothes put me on the tree and let go. I flew for a long ways and I landed in a swamp. Then I came here.

You could hear a pin drop for a whole minute.

Finally Mr. Canton spoke up.

"You crazy or drunk, Mister?"

"I'm telling you the truth"

"You know, Ralf, I've heard of stories, about these green men before."

"That's right" said another.

"Next thing you will believe the stories about the witch too" said Mr. Canton.

"Witch?" asked Jamison.

"Sure, they say she lives up there on the mountain, no one goes up there without her knowing it"

"I'm not going up there no more" said Jamison

"Just what were you doing up there, mister?" asked one.

Jamison decided to tell part of the truth.

85

"I was hunting for that Indian gold"

"That's a rumor; the only thing up there is the old Indian burial mounds."

"I've heard that the place is haunted. Stay away from there" said another.

"All I want to do is get cleaned up and head back to Georgia" said Jamison.

But before he did, old ways came back; he broke into a store, but was caught and was now in the local pokey.

That evening in walked Johnson, covered with mud.

"Here's another one" said one of the men to Mr. Canton.

"Over here" pointed Mr. Canton to a chair and table?

"Ma"

"I'm bringing it" said Ma.

After drinking the whisky he started to tell his story.

"Let me guess, something hit you on the head and then you flew through the air, landed in a swamp and came here" said Mr. Canton

Johnson just looked at him, how did he know that?

"Except I hit a tree, my head hurts something bad" said Johnson.

"We had a feller come through this morning with the same story" said Mr. Canton.

"That must have been Jamison, he disappeared first"

"Bob, come over here" said Mr. Canton.

Bob was the county Sheriff who had stopped by the Inn to say hello to some of his friends. When he walked up to the table, Johnson tried to squeeze down in the chair.

"What's up Ralf?" asked Bob.

"Something funny going on here, Bob, we've had two men come down the mountain in this shape with the same story."

"OK, fella, out with it, or you're going to spend the night or more in the Pokey"

Johnson told the truth this time, about the children, the map and the gold. He also told about the others that were still up there after them.

"Bob, we can't leave the children up there. We have to do something" said Ralf.

"I know, it's only one man and four children against hardened crooks"

"I'm going to take this fella over to the jail to join his friend and when I come back we need to get some men together and leave in the morning."

"Come on" said the Sheriff.

"I didn't do anything" said Johnson.

"You might have somewhere else"

The Sheriff took him over to the jail and locked him up.

He then went to the Inn and along with Ralf and some others made arraignments to leave first thing in the mourning.

CHAPTER EIGHT

"I would like to dig those mounds up to see what's in them" said Sam.

Just then a Screech Owl sounded.

All of them jumped almost out of their skins.

"I don't think they would like that" said Picket

"We don't have time" said Jack.

They were standing in front of the cave looking up at the skull carved in the face of the mountain.

"I never have seen anything like this before" said Sam.

"It just means there's got to be gold in there" said Jack.

These men had come prepared, some had flashlights, and some had lanterns.

They turned on the flashlights and lit the lanterns.

"Look here, there are footprints" said Jack.

"Piece of cake from here on" said Jack.

With that they went inside. They followed the footsteps of the children and Tom. They had in there for about half and hour when Pruitt spoke up.

"There's someone else in here besides us."

"Of course there is stupid, the children and the man" answered Sam

"No, not them, something else, can't you feel it?"

"You're just hala hootnating" said Jack.

"I'm not; I went before we came in"

"No, not that, it means you are seeing things" said Jack.

"I don't think so, there's something in here besides us"

Later on, when deeper into the cave, Picket spoke up.

"Hey fellas, I think Sam is right, I keep seeing the Shadows following us"

"I told you" said Pruitt.

"Stop it, let's go" said Jack.

"Booom!!"

The concussion was so loud it just about blew out the eardrums of the men. The loud firing of the rifle echoed off the walls.

"God man, don't fire that rifle in here again" shouted Jack.

He couldn't hear himself talk for his ears were ringing so badly.

In fact all of them had their hands to their ears.

"But I saw something" said Pruitt.

"Did it have a gun or knife?" asked Jack.

"No"

"Then for God's sake, don't shoot that thing again, unless you see it with one"

The men, with ears still ringing, moved on down the cave.

The sound of the rifle being fired caught

up with James and the children.

"There's an earthquake coming!" said Boob.

"That wasn't an earthquake, Boob that was a rifle shot" said James.

"Rifle shot?" asked Sidney.

"There's someone following us."

"What are we going to do?" asked Sidney

"We will go on, but be on the lookout for them"

"Stay close together" ordered James.

The little men stood in front of the cave entrance.

"This is it; we have no lights to go in. Let's go back and tell Glenna"

Glenna knew they were coming before they came across the field and up to the house. She was waiting for them on the porch.

"Sorry, Glenna, we got two but the rest made it into the cave."

"You did well and I'm proud of you, there is evil on this mountain and I feel now that the spirits of the mountain will have to protect the children, and James."

"Come on in, get something to eat, you did well and you must be hungry." she said.

While they went in, she stood on the porch looking up at the mountain and said a little prayer for them.

"I'm tired" said Boob

"You're right; we have been going for a

while. Let's stop here for the night." said Tom.

It wasn't hard to find some wood; the floor was covered in it. It was old, a lot older than them. It made good kindle for the fire.

"Think they will find us?" asked Sidney.

"Not tonight, they have to stop too, I think they are far enough behind us we don't have to worry tonight." said James.

At least that's what he told them. He was worried. He had no idea who was behind them but the fact that someone was following them was a bad omen. And he didn't know how many there were of them. He would trust the spirits of the cave to watch over them.

After eating they all fell asleep around the fire.

During the night the wood had burned faster then expected and it went out. They were in the dark, at least that's what they thought.

"Look" said Elijah looking around him.

"My God" said Boob.

"What's happening?" asked Aubrey.

The cave walls gave off an eerie light. They were glowing.

The cave had a light green glow in it. You could see without the fire or torches.

"I've seen this before when I saw some seaweed glow in the ocean."

"They called it Phosphorus; it's caused by some chemical in the stone"

"It's spooky" said Boob.

"I think it's pretty" said Sidney.

"Someone or something is looking out for us, our torches would not have lasted much longer" said James.

"Now we can continue without worrying about light"

They left the camp and headed deeper into the cave.

It was easier this time.

Where the torches only gave light around them for a few feet, the cave now was well lit.

The group of men was waking up. They had yet to discover the secret of the cave walls.

They still had plenty of fuel for their lanterns.

They started out after the little group and the gold.

While walking in line one behind the other.

"You know, I'm still going to open one of those Indian mounds when we leave." said Sam.

"I never liked any stinking Indians" he said.

"Only good Indian is a dead Indian"

As soon as he said that, something began to happen.

The Shadows started moving, moving toward the group.

"What the...." said Jack.

In front of the men appeared two Shadow figures with glowing red eyes. They floated toward them with arms outstretched.

"I think they are coming after you Sam" said Jack.

"You shouldn't have said those things, not in here"

Sam started running back toward the front of the cave. He was running as fast as he could.

The Shadow men went by Picket and Jack towards Sam. Each got on one side and appeared to take his arms and lift him off the ground. All of them disappeared into the dark.

"He.....lp...Me...!" screamed Sam.

Then there was silence.

"My God" said Picket.

"Let's get out of here" said Pruitt.

"No, we are close to that gold. Sam was not smart. This means we split the gold only three ways." said Jack.

"Maybe less" said Picket.

"Come on" said Jack. They left and continued on. They were not the same. Each one was thinking of what had happened to Sam. It made them uneasy.

But it didn't stop the urge for the gold, nothing would stop that.

All Sam remembered was that he was lifted up and it became dark. Then it was daylight and he was outside the mountain. It didn't look like the same path he and the others had come up on.

Deer and other animals came to the edge of the path and looked at him. These deer were not afraid of him; in fact they looked at him like he was totally new.

Further down the mountain he stopped. He saw a village in front of him. It was an Indian village. It was not like the ones he had seen pictures of drawn by early explorers of the America's west. He must have something wrong with him, maybe he hit his head. This wasn't possible.

Then it struck him, he looked around and saw the burial mounds. These were the same mounds in front of the cave.

It couldn't be because there was no Indian village there.

He walked on and into the village. This wasn't like he thought an Indian village would be like, instead of the teepee's, it was a well laid out village of log cabins, some having the skins of animals nailed to the front.

Out of one came an old man. Sam walked up to him.

"We were expecting you" the old man said

"Expecting me?" asked Sam.

"Yes the Spirits told us you were coming"

"The Spirits?"

"The ones who brought you here"

"But how, why?"

"Come in, I will explain"

Sam went in and found that a table and chairs where there for them to sit. They were made out of wood from the forest.

"How do you speak English so well" asked Sam

"We speak our language, Tsalagi; you are made to understand it."

"You were brought here to learn about our culture, to live it, to understand it"

The old man explained that they had been here since the early 1800s and the village was of the Cherokee Nation. Some of his People had escaped the forced move to Oklahoma.

Since then they have lived in a magical valley in the mountains. No one would find them unless they wanted them too.

The Cherokee had once lived in the mountains from Virginia to Georgia. They had been called Chiluk-ki by the Choctaws, meaning cave People. The cave he had been in was a sacred cave. No evil that enters will remain there. That's why he was brought here.

"You will remain with us for a while"

"First we have to find you a place to live"

"Look, I'm not staying here, I'm...."

The old man raised his hand and spoke, "It is decided"

He took Sam outside and walked him over to a cabin by the woods. Out came a woman about his age.

"This is Orenda; she has no one to look out for her, stay here"

So it came to pass that Sam stayed there and helped her.

Her name was Awentia, Fawn, and he fell in love.

He learned to hunt with the younger males of the village. He learned how to skin and cook deer, rabbit, squirrel, and other forest creatures.

They had one son, Tayanita, Young Beaver. He grew up to be brave and strong.

In this land the Indians didn't have to fear the white men, they simply were not around. It was as the old man had said; this village was in a magical land. He grew older and older.

His wife had died years earlier and now he was preparing to go. His son was at his side.

"Father, you have been good, it is time for you to go ahead, and your name will be remembered in the village for all times"

Sam went to sleep.

The Sheriff and a few men from town had been on the trail up the mountain. They brought Johnson with them to identify the others who were after the children.

It was midmorning when they saw a man walking down the mountain toward them.

He looked like a man who was not from here. He had on old style Indian clothes. His hair was white, and it was long, pony tail, down past his shoulders.

He had aged many years.

"Sam?" asked Johnson.

"Sam, that you?" he said again.

Sam looked at him with wide eyes and mumbled.

"I've been gone for twenty years." said Sam.

"That's crazy, Sam, it's only been a few days"

"No, I've been to a village, an Indian village, very old; I've been there for twenty years. I had a wife and child. I went to sleep and now I'm here."

"Sam it's only been two days" said Johnson.

"No, I must go, I have things to do, to make things right." he said.

"Make things right?" asked Johnson.

"Yes, we did the Indians wrong, I must tell them, and I have to go"

Sam turned away from them and headed down the mountain.

"How could he have aged like that?" asked one of the men.

"They are strange things that happen in these mountains. Some you can't explain, this is one of them" said the Sheriff.

The posse headed on up the mountain, wondering what they would run into next.

"Look over there" said Sidney pointing to

something shining on the ground. They walked over to it and looked down.

"What is it?" asked Elijah.

"It's a skeleton" said Boob.

"Looks what he is wearing" said Aubrey.

It was a strange sight, the skeleton of a man wearing a silver breast plate.

"There's his helmet" said Sidney.

By its skull was a silver helmet with the front rising up in a point above the forehead.

"Its armor, a breastplate worn by the conquistadors" answered James.

"Look at his hand" said Aubrey.

The arm was stretched out and the index finger of his right hand was pointing in the direction of the wall in front of them.

"What is he pointing at?" asked Sidney.

"Let's go see" said James.

There was an opening in the wall that led to another chamber in the cave.

"Let's see where this leads" said James.

"I don't know it looks spooky to me" said Elijah.

"Everything looks spooky to you" said Boob.

James didn't wait, he went in. That left the children outside all alone. They looked at each other and then ran through the entrance.

James was standing there looking straight ahead, not saying a word.

In front of them was a rock alter with piles of gold plated cups, dishes, chains, crosses and many, many more items.

Lying on the ground in front of the alter, were two other skeletons.

Each had bags of gold and silver around them.

"They never made it out." said James.

"I guess the story is true, three men came in and none left."

"They came with evil in their minds"

Said a voice out of the dark.

All of them jumped. They looked in the direction that the voice came from.

An old Indian of long time ago was standing there.

He was the same Indian that Sam had seen in the village. James and the children just stood there, frozen still.

"Don't be afraid, I know why you came and I know why others follow you.

You, young man have a good heart, you came only to help these children, that is good, and you children come to find hope"

"Let me tell you a story." the old man started.

"These men came here a long time ago after they had stolen from our People. They came here after torturing an Indian to death to tell them of this place. He was a good man, but young, he didn't have the strength not to give in. They came for evil, for greed. They found their gold but it did them no good, for there they lay. Now you have come and evil has

99

followed you."

"We didn't know that, mister" said Boob.

"I know that child, that's why I have let you come in".

"This here is all our treasures. We gathered it together, throughout the nations of our Peoples and brought it here.

It does not mean the same for us as you.

It is our heritage. This is our past. We are here to protect it."

"We didn't know. We came here for greed too."

"We are sorry" said James.

"It is alright, we see into your hearts, you meant good by it, not evil" said the old man.

The Indian walked toward them, bent down and picked up something that looked like marbles.

He walked over to James and gave them to him. James put them in his pocket.

"I am giving these to you; I want you to take them. Use them for good. Some of our People are in need too, go help them, give them the money to build homes, to eat and raise children."

"Also, take some with you, help the little ones, they are brave, they need help too. You will find your answer with the women in the meadow, she is good, and she needs a good man. Go to her."

The children giggled at that.

"I will show you the way, follow me."

While James and the children were following the old man out of the cave, Jack and his group were nearing the place where the skeleton was seen.

The light from the lantern was shining on the silver breastplate.

"Look!" shouted Picket.

They saw the skeleton laying there with his finger pointing in the same direction.

"Here it is"

Jack said finding the entrance to the inner room.

"Would you look at that." said Jack.

"I told you it was here" he said.

"Grab some of those bags and load up" said Pruitt.

The men loaded as much as they could carry.

They put the bags over their backs and started out the same way they came in.

The old man was leading James and the children, so he wasn't there to stop them.

After a short walk through the tunnel they came out into sunlight.

"You must not tell anyone about this cave and the room"

"Il won't" said James.

"I swear, I swear" said the children crossing their hearts.

The old Indian smiled.

"I have faith in you, do as I have asked

and you will have a long and joyful life, and now go.

The evil men have found the room. I must go"

James had walked a little ways and looked back. He couldn't see the entrance to the tunnel, it was solid rock. The Indian was gone too.

Jack and his men had made it out of the cave.

"Wait a minute" said Jack.

"What?" asked Picket?

"The children were not there" said Jack.

"Where?"

"The gold room, they were not there"

"That's right"

"That means they got out and have more gold" said Jack.

"So"

"We can't let them get away; they know where the gold is."

"We have to kill them so we are the only ones who know."

"That way it's only ours, no one else can find out and go get It." said Jack.

"That's right, this is just the first trip." said Pruitt.

"There must be another exit; we have to go find them"

"How?"

"Go around the mountain, they have to be heading toward the valley." said Jack.

They headed to the valley, Glenna's valley. They had to stop the children and James.

James and the children started walking down the mountain toward the valley where Glenna lived.

It was late evening and they had to stop for the night.

"There's is an open grassy area and a stream over there." said James.

The camp fire was going, the group had settled down after eating a meal of beans and hard biscuits.

"I sure will be glad when we get to Miss Glenna's" said Elijah.

"Me too" said Aubrey.

"I kind of miss her too" said James.

The children looked at each other thinking.

"I just bet he does." whispered Boob.

"You know children, no one will believe you if you tell this story.

"We have to respect other people's beliefs, faiths and their way of life. I think by this, we have found a certain type of treasure, don't you?" said James.

Sidney spoke up first.

"I think you are right, I will not tell anyone what happened. I will devote my life to doing good deeds. I love this mountain and I don't want to ever leave it."

She then looked at the boys.

103

"You better not ever say anything about this or I will bury my fist in your heads"

The boys were shocked, what had gotten into Sidney. She talked liked an adult, a grown up women. They knew she meant it. Although none would say out loud, they all loved her; they would do nothing to hurt her. And nobody else will hurt her; after all she was their Sidney.

"We won't" repeated the boys.

"We have to still be careful, the men are out there and there's no telling what they will do." said James.

CHAPTER NINE

Not far away camped Jack, Pruitt and Picket. They were camped along the same creek, about one mile up the mountain.

"You think they went this way?" asked Picket.

"Sure, it's the only way to go. This leads off the mountain to the valley" said Jack.

They were camped underneath some tall pine trees.

All of them were excited by the gold that they had in their packs.

"Look at this one" said Pruitt holding up a gold plate.

"I bet it's worth a thousand dollars" he smiled

"Yea, look at this" said Picket showing a gold necklace.

"Put that away, we have plenty of time for that, first we must stop the children and get their gold." said Jack.

"You think we will catch up with them in the morning?" asked Picket.

"By the afternoon."

"The children can't walk as far or as long as us" said Jack.

Out of the dark came the wail of a Screech Owl.

"God, I hate that sound" said Pruitt.

"Look" said Picket.

Up on a limb of the tree near them sat a

Screech Owl. It was grey and had green eyes.

"Would you look at that, I've never seen one with green eyes" said Picket.

"They don't, it's just the light from the fire" said Jack.

"Well, I'm going to stop that screeching now" said Pruitt.

Before they could stop him, Picket took up his rifle and fired at the owl.

"Ha, Ha, Ha You missed him" laughed Jack

"Not this time" said Picket raising his rifle up again.

Before he could fire the growl of a bear came out from the woods near them.

"Jesus!" said Jack.

The growl got louder and louder.

"He's coming this way!" yelled Picket.

Before the men could move to get their weapons the bear broke through the bushes and ran straight at Picket.

Picket took off running as fast as he could.

The bear, the biggest they had ever seen, ran through the camp and after him. Back down the trail they had just come over.

"What are we going to do?" asked Picket.

"What can we do, did you see the size of that thing" answered Jack.

"What about Pruitt"

"He's on his on"

106

"Anyway he left his share of the gold. If he doesn't come back by the morning it's ours" smiled Jack.

"God, what a way to go" said Picket.

"It was either him or us" said Jack.

The ways of evil men don't change; it's always everyone for himself.

Especially when it came to gold.

Pruitt was running as hard as he could but he couldn't lose that bear. He ran through briars, hitting tree stumps, he was giving out of breath.

Out of energy he tripped and fell and turned over and looked that bear in the eyes. He knew he was dead. The bear didn't eat him. He stood over him with both his front legs on the sides of his body.

The bear looked him in the eyes. Something happened to Pruitt, he was being told to leave the forest. He was not wanted here. Just before he left the bear make a swipe at his face, leaving a sign on his face.

Then the bear left. Watching him leave Pruitt saw that one minute the bear was there and the next he wasn't. He was gone.

Pruitt got up and started walking the other way down the mountain. He didn't care about any gold, all he wanted to do was leave, leave this mountain and the bear.

Jack and Picket were up early the next morning.

"He didn't come back" said Picket.

"Grab his gold, we'll spit it later" said Jack.

"I've been thinking, let's cut around and meet them at he bottom of the hill." said Jack.

"Now you'll talking, Lets go" answered Picket.

"Who it that?" asked the Sheriff.

"That's Pruitt" said Johnson

The Sheriff's posse stopped and waited for Pruitt to come up to them. His clothes were torn and he had scratches on his face.

The scratches looked like a bear paw.

Ok, mister, tell me what has happened?" asked the Sheriff.

"We were following the children; Jack wants to kill them, to get their gold. I was attacked by a bear.

"I'm going" said Pruitt.

"There really is gold up there?" asked one of the men.

Pruitt thought about the bear, he didn't want anyone hunting the gold.

"No, Jack just thinks there is, he thinks the children and that man has some, never seen none." said Pruitt.

The gold fever of the men died. This man was talking about bears.

He is crazy. They all thought.

"Bart, you and Slim, take this man back to the station house, clean him up, and lock him up. We will check on his status later." said the sheriff.

108

"Wait!" shouted the Sheriff to Pruitt.

"Which way were you going?"

"Down the valley"

"How many are left?"

"Two, Jack and Picket"

Bart and Slim led Pruitt down to the town, where he would join Jamison and Johnson.

"Come on men, we have to hurry, this Jack is mean, we have to get there before he kills someone." said the Sheriff.

"Did you see that scratch on his face" said one of the men.

"Something is happening out there, what I don't know, but something strange" said another.

"Here they come" said Picket in a low voice to Jack.

The children and James were walking down the path when out from behind some rocks came Jack and Picket.

"Gotch ya" said Picket.

They had both rifles pointing at the group.

"Tie them up" ordered Jack.

James lunged at Jack, but before he could get to him, Picket fired.

James fell to the ground.

"Did you kill him?" asked Jack.

"Naw, just winged him"

James got up; he was shot in the left shoulder.

Sidney ran over, tore her shirt from the bottom and pressed it to his shoulder, stopping the bleeding.

"That's good, missy, keep him alive, at least for a while, now tie them up."

James was first in line, with the children tied with a rope running from one to the other, with their hands tied behind their backs.

They walked behind Jack with Picket following in the rear with his rifle.

They were going back to the cave. Jack figured that was the perfect place to get rid of the bodies.

The posse had reached the spot where the children were captured.

"Look here" said one of the men pointing to the ground.

"Looks like blood" said another.

"Charlie, the best tracker, come over here, look at this" said the Sheriff.

Charlie walked over to the spot and looked down, moved around the area and said,

"One was shot, looks like he made an attempt to stop them. A little one with small footprints came up to help. They used cloth, see the little pieces there." he pointed.

"The way they are walking they are tied up; see the footprints, one behind the other. They're heading back to the cave."

"Back to the cave?" asked one man.

"To get rid of the bodies, it's a perfect place." said the Sheriff.

"We have to walk fast and into the night, no stopping, let's hope we get there in time." said the Sheriff.

"If we don't they're mine" said another.

"Me too" said the rest. No one was going to kill children in these mountains.

There was unwritten law in the mountains.

You could shoot your best friend, but no one, no one hurts children.

It was a long walk for them. James was grunting now and then from the pain. Sidney would turn around and look back at him and then look at the men. If looks could kill, those two would be in hell by now. Yes sir that was one strong girl. Boob, Elijah and Aubrey were just about worn out, walking like this, up hill and tied, took all your energy.

It was now night time. Jack and Picket had lit the lanterns. That caused light and Shadows to be thrown across the land as they walked.

"We're here" said Jack.

"I don't know about this." said Picket.

"Don't worry about it, once we're done, it will not bother you anymore" said Jack.

When they got to the alter, they sat the children and James down in front of it.

The glow from the lanterns flickered light around the room.

"Let's get this over with" said Jack, raising his rifle.

Boob, Aubrey and Elijah had tears in their eyes. Sidney just stared them down; she didn't even turn her head.

James spoke up.

"You think you can get away with this?"

"Sure, I have before" replied Jack.

"What about Glenna, she knows we are up here, she will know."

"No problem, I'll take care of her too"

Jack raised his rifle again.

"I don't know I never killed children" said Picket.

"I'll do it" said Jack.

The lantern blew out. It was total darkness.

"What the..?" said Jack.

The cave came to light with glowing rocks; it had a green color to it.

"Jack, Jack" said Picket.

"I see them." said Jack.

Around the room stood Indians.

All had either bows and arrows or spears.

In front of the children and Tom, stood one very old Indian. He spoke.

"There will be no killing here today"

"And who are you?" asked Jack.

"I am the protector of this place; no harm will be done here"

"I don't like this, let's get out of here" said Picket and started to leave.

Two Indians stepped in front of him.

They took his weapon out of his hands. Picket turned around and stood beside Jack.

Jack raised his rifle to shoot the old man, when an arrow flew out, hit his hand, causing the rifle to drop.

Boob, Aubrey and Elijah were smiling, Sidney was still staring at Jack.

"You have brought evil to this place; you will now pay for doing so."

"Take them" said the old man.

The Indians didn't move. There came a low moaning sound, and then out of the shadows came the Shadow People. All had red glowing eyes. They gathered around Jack and Picket, lifted them off their feet and disappeared with them down the dark tunnel. They were screaming all the way.

The old Indian walked over to James and the children and untied them.

James was weak from lost of blood, he had to sit down.

The old man pointed. An Indian brought a cup filled with some liquid. James took it and drank from it, it did help.

"It will give you strength"

"You are brave, we watched you, trying to save the young ones. You are welcome anytime. And you young maiden, you have courage, you will do to ride the river with. Now, it is over. Go to the valley."

"What will happen to them" asked James.

113

"They have been taken back to the village.

They have many years to change, and they will, we have our ways." said the old man.

James and the children were walking back toward the entrance to the cave; he wanted to ask another question. When he looked back, they were gone.

"Where did he go?" asked Boob.

"He went back to a better place and time" said James.

CHAPTER TEN

They walked back outside. Sidney was holding on to him, helping him along the way.

"It's dark, we can't see where to go" said Boob.

"We can't stop, Big Cat needs help" said Sidney.

"Oh, Glenna, where are you, we need your help" she said in a whispered prayer.

A strange thing began to happen. Out of no where came thousands of Lightning Bugs. I mean thousands.

They were standing in front of the cave entrance looking down the path in front of the burial mounds. The lightning bugs were spread out along that path, lighting the way, as if telling them to follow.

"Follow the signs, thought James. That's what Glenna said."

"Follow the signs?" Boob asked.

"Let's go" said James.

"Go where?" asked Sidney.

"Follow them" he said as he pointed to the Lightning Bugs

As they walked the Lightning Bugs moved ahead of them, lighting and showing them the way. It was magical.

People in the valley saw a very strange sight that night.

If you looked up at the mountain you would see a long light weaving its way from the top of the mountain to the valley.

The light moved in and out of trees, over streams and finally disappeared at the valley of the witch.

Glenna was on her porch watching the light come down the mountain and finally into the field in front of her house.

When the lightning bugs got there they flew up in the air in all directions.

For a moment it looked like fireworks. A big bright exploding light and then it was gone.

Glenna saw Sidney holding on to James, brave Sidney. Even if she was as tired as the boys, she would not let go of James. She guided him to the porch.

"I have him now Sidney, go inside, there is some food on the table."

Glenna put her arm underneath James and helped him through the door.

Later all the children were laying on couches and chairs, all asleep, just plain worn out.

Glenna took James over by the wood burning stove.

She had some hot water in a pot where there was some were some special herbs, needed for healing the wound.

She sat him down in a chair and started working on it. Soon she had him patched up with a cloth tied around the area.

"Thank You" said James.

"No, thank you, for looking out for the

children."

"I have a story to tell you"

"I know it already, it was meant to be" she said

"Meant to be?"

"Yes, the old Indian had told me years ago a man was coming, a good man, who was lost and he would bring surprises to my life."

"I guess the surprises were the children" she continued.

"You knew?"

"He said it was meant to be"

"Who am I to question him" answered James.

They laughed together.

He fell asleep in that chair.

Glenna put covers over the children and kept checking on James for fever.

She stayed there all night.

The dawn broke peaceful and calm. The children were up and moving about. Glenna had made them take baths, for they were very dirty. The children had met the little men and were out with them learning several circus tricks. You could hear their laughter all around the valley. It sounded nice and natural to Glenna.

Around noon a man riding a horse came into the valley and up to Glenna's house. It was the Sheriff.

Glenna and James came out onto the porch.

He had his arm in a sling.

The Sheriff saw this and winced. He got down off his house and walked up to them.

"I tried to get there. When we got to the cave all we found were the hats that belonged to Jack and Picket."

The children came running around the house yelling and screaming with joy.

"Seems like they came out alright" said the Sheriff.

"Young ones get over things sooner than us, Sheriff." said Glenna.

"One day I will come back to hear the story, of course I won't believe it."

"I come about these children, you know they ran away from the orphanage in Georgia, I have papers for them." said the Sheriff.

"Oh, no" said Glenna.

"Now, Now, you know me Glenna, I knew your mom, she did things for this valley that many have forgotten, but I have not."

"You know us mountain People look at things differently."

"If I took these young'uns back to the orphanage, no telling what would happen to them, now if they had a good home and a good mother and father, I don't see any harm in saying I couldn't find them. You know a lot of strange things go on in these mountains, who knows what happened to them"

"Oh, Sheriff, I will be a good mother and James will be a good father, we will raise them as our own." said Glenna.

"What about you James?" asked the Sheriff.

He looked at Glenna and said,

"I reckon so Sheriff" and smiled.

"Now we need to get them to school and you two married. Let me know when you set the date, I'll come back and hear that story."

"We will and it will be soon" said Glenna.

"I know the judge in town, we will also figure a way for you to adopt them." said the Sheriff.

"You know the judge?" asked James.

"Yep, he's my brother, see ya later" said the Sheriff getting on his horse.

He was sitting there and said.

"Yes indeed, strange things happen in these mountains."

He smiled, turned his horse and left.

EPILOGUE

Back at the jail sat Johnson, Jamison and Pruitt. They had some old warrants on them from Georgia. They were waiting to be picked up.

"Man, I was a fool for listening to Jack." said Johnson.

"You are telling me." Said Jamison.

It was late at night the full moon was shinning through the window of the cell.

"He doesn't ever move" said Jamison talking about Pruitt lying on his bed.

A cry came out from the mountain, it rolled on down the hills through the town. It was the cry of the bear on the mountain.

Pruitt jumped up and stared.

He still had the mark of the bear on his cheek.

"It's alright, he can't get in here" said Johnson.

"Don't be so sure" answered Pruitt.

"Don't be so sure" he said again.

That Fall James and Glenna did get married. Though some funny paperwork the children were adopted.

Sidney grew up to be quite a witch herself. Glenna taught her about herbs and healing. She went to medical school and became a doctor. She wanted to help the mountain people.

Aubrey became a lawyer.

Elijah loved the new cars and became the best mechanic in the hills.

Boob went off and joined the circus. Later he became part owner of one.

Tom and Glenna lived the rest of their lives out in the valley.

The house was empty. It had been for many years. Sidney had come back with her husband and her children. She moved her practice to town.

The boys were here too, all drawn back to this place.

All had settled in the valley. All had families. Something had happened to them here, something special, that drew them back.

Sidney's husband was out and about the place with her brothers and their children.

With the shade cooling the front porch steps Sidney sat with her youngest daughter, Glenna Ann.

She is about Sidney's age when she had first come here. They were on the porch looking out within the Shadow of the mountain. Sidney put her arm around her and said,

"Let me tell you the story about Bear Holler Mountain......"